Gyles Brandreth

JOKE BOX

Illustrated by Tony Blundell

Puffin Books

Puffin Books, Penguin Books Ltd, Harmondsworth, Middlesex, England
Viking Penguin Inc., 40 West 23rd Street, New York, New York 10010, U.S.A.
Penguin Books Australia Ltd, Ringwood, Victoria, Australia
Penguin Books Canada Limited, 2801 John Street, Markham, Ontario,
Canada L3R 1B4
Penguin Books (N.Z.) Ltd, 182–190 Wairau Road, Auckland 10, New Zealand

First published 1986

Made and printed in Great Britain by
Cox & Wyman Ltd, Reading
Filmset in Linotron Palatino by
Rowland Phototypesetting Ltd,
Bury St Edmunds, Suffolk

Puffin Books

JOKE BOX

Why is it that the same joke can make one person roll around the floor in hysterics, while another person simply groans at its awfulness? What *is* it about jokes that makes them funny? In *Joke Box* expert jokesmith Gyles Brandreth gets to the bottom of the subject!

From 'Knock, knock' and 'Waiter, waiter' jokes, via 'April Fools' and 'Spoonerisms', to wisecracks, X certificates and many, many more! With hundreds of jokes for you to practise on your friends, and lots of useful tips for making up – and telling – your *own* jokes, this book contains everything an aspiring comic could want to know!

Happy joke-cracking!

Gyles Brandreth is the author of many books of quizzes, puzzles, games and jokes. He is also a well-known children's television personality. He lives in London with his wife and three children.

Dedicated to my distant cousins and close friends:
Rosa Carrots, Thayer Thorry, Della Katessen, Felix Ited,
Lydia Dustbin, Constance Norah, Eliza Wake, Willy
Makit and Lucy Lastick.

Contents

1 What is a Joke?

What is a joke?

Quite simply, a joke is something said – or done – to cause amusement. Some jokes, of course, are a lot funnier than others. Some will make you smile, some will make you chuckle, some will make you laugh out loud, a lot will make you groan and a few (a very few) will have you rolling around on the floor in a state of happy hysteria.

Jokes come in all shapes and sizes, so let's begin by looking at a variety of different types of joke to see if we can discover how each type works and what makes it funny. Here is an old favourite:

How do you cure water on the brain?
With a tap on the head.

It is a joke based on the *pun*, a form of wordplay which depends on words that sound (and sometimes are) the same, but which have completely different meanings. With this particular joke the pun word, of course, is 'tap', which can mean either a device for regulating the flow of water or a gentle knock. Many, many jokes, including almost all those of the 'knock, knock' variety (see Chapter 3), are based on puns. Take a look at these three:

Why did the bank robber have a bath?
So he could make a clean getaway.

Two buckets were sitting chatting to each other. Said the first bucket to the second, 'You don't look like a well bucket to me.'

Said the second to the first, 'You're quite right, I am feeling a little pail.'

How do you treat a pig with a sore throat?
You give it oinkment.

In the first two examples, ordinary words are used in such a way that people deliberately 'misunderstand' their meaning, i.e. 'clean', 'well' and 'pail'. With the third example, the pun is taken a step further and a nonsense word is invented which sounds very much like the real word – 'ointment – oinkment' – but which incorporates the noise a pig makes, 'oink'. It would be no use saying, 'How do you treat a dog with a sore throat?' and giving the same reply.

You will find lots of jokes in this book based on puns, most notably those in the Dizzy Dictionary (Chapter 19, page 120). Here is a list of words that lend themselves to making puns. Try to make up some jokes of your own based on them.

anti/auntie
bare/bear
carat/carrot
dear/deer
eerie/eyrie
Fred/thread
guessed/guest
hoarse/horse
I/eye
jest/just
knight/night
light (not heavy/not dark)
made/maid
nanny (nursemaid/female goat)
oil/all
place/plaice
quack/crack
rock (a stone/to go to and fro)
seas/seize
train (to educate/a locomotive)
urn/earn
verse/worse
won/one
you/ewe
zinc/sink/think

Many of the most popular jokes are based on puns, but by no means all. Some of the finest jokes involve *mistakes* and *misunderstandings*, and Chapter 4 is full of them. Some people say funny things without meaning to. For example, my wife once said to me: 'Fry the baby while I feed the sausages'! Or the mistake can result from mud-dled thinking, such as, 'Joan of Arc was Noah's daughter.' Mistakes can occur in written form, too, and you will find lots of these in Chapter 12.

Allied to muddled thinking is a kind of joke which I find very funny, as it has behind it a glorious kind of nonsense logic:

FOREMAN: Why are you only carrying one plank at a time when everyone else is carrying two?
WORKER: *They're too lazy to make a double journey like I do.*

Another popular kind of joke is the *wisecrack*. You need to be very quick-witted to make quips like these:

MR JONES: Did any of your family ever make a brilliant marriage?
MR SMITH: *Only my wife.*

MRS JONES: Whenever I'm down in the dumps I buy myself a new hat.
MRS SMITH: *So that's where you get them!*

The jokes are funny because they are clever and insulting, though if you ever make any yourself you have to remember to be very careful not to be too rude or unpleasant about people. You will find more wisecracks in Chapter 11.

A category of joke which people find extremely funny is the *nonsense* joke, and the supreme nonsense joke is the elephant joke:

How do you get four elephants in a Mini?
Two in the front and two in the back.

Elephant and other nonsense jokes are funny because they are so absurd. And again, they have a wonderfully crazy logic about them – after all, how else would you get four elephants in a Mini? You will find a whole chapter devoted to elephant jokes if you turn to page 36.

At the opposite end of the scale to elephant jokes are those we call *sick jokes*, that is, jokes that are rather nasty or vulgar. They really ought to make us shudder, but instead they make us giggle. It's the same reaction we have when, after talking in the daylight about ghosts, we find ourselves in a dark room and the door opens silently and unexpectedly. For example:

'Mummy, what is a vampire?'
'Shut up and drink your soup before it clots.'

If you like this kind of joke then you will find it in Chapter 17, but if you are rather a sensitive sort of person then you should perhaps give that chapter a miss!

And yet another category of joke makes us laugh because it takes us by *surprise*. Look at these examples:

A man had spent some time sorting out a complicated and expensive insurance policy to protect his home. Just as the broker was leaving, he asked yet another question.

'What would I get if the house were to burn down tonight?'

The broker looked at him. 'About ten years, I should think,' he replied.

A very attractive girl went into a dress shop. She tried on almost all the dresses they had, but could find nothing to suit her. Then she had an idea. 'Could I try on that dress in the window?' she asked.

'I wish you would,' said the assistant. 'It would be very good for business.'

The first is a rather sophisticated joke based on the fact that if the man's house were to be damaged he would be paid money in compensation. He is referring to the money when he asks, 'What would I get?', but the broker is referring to the fact that he might burn down the house deliberately just to claim the money – which would be a criminal offence – hence his reply.

In the second joke the ending is not what we expect, either, and so we laugh.

And in a way the jokes are a little like puns, too, in that the second person has a different interpretation of an idea from that of the first person.

As you can see, there are many different ways of creating a funny joke. But if you want to tell jokes of your own and succeed in making other people laugh you also need to have an eye for a funny situation and a sense of timing – that vital ingredient in every comedian's act. You will find more about how to tell jokes in the next chapter.

If you are serious about humour (and that is not a contradiction in terms!), then it is a very good idea to keep a notebook to hand at all times to jot down funny things you hear and see. You can also use it to note down jokes other people tell you, otherwise you are bound to forget the punchlines at the vital moment!

This book has another twenty-three chapters about jokes and humour, among which you will find old favourites like doctor jokes and waiter jokes, and many more that may be new to you. There are also chapters on practical jokes and funny rhymes, and there's even one that shows you how to make a clown costume and funny masks, and teaches you how to do simple ventriloquism. In each of the chapters about types of jokes I have tried to explain what makes that particular type funny, to help you to create some for yourself. But the real test of any joke is whether it makes you laugh. I hope those in the *Joke Box* do.

2 How To Tell Jokes

Although all the really funny comedians seem to tell the first jokes that come into their heads and make everyone roll about with hysterical laughter, successful joke telling isn't that simple. To make people laugh requires a considerable amount of serious preparation and forethought.

Before I explain any more about how to tell jokes and make people laugh I am going to give you Brandreth's Seven Golden Rules of Successful Joke Telling. They are printed in bold, black capital letters to make them easy to read and learn off by heart.

The most vital thing to remember about telling jokes is **NEVER START TELLING A JOKE UNLESS YOU ARE SURE YOU CAN REMEMBER ALL OF IT, ESPECIALLY THE PUNCHLINE.** This rule applies particularly to shaggy dog stories – see Chapter 10 – but even short jokes can be ruined by saying the wrong word at the wrong time. Take this 'doctor' joke:

'Doctor, doctor, I keep thinking I'm a goat.'
'How long has this been going on?'
'Ever since I was a kid.'

Suppose someone started to tell it without remembering it properly, and they said, 'Ever since I was a child,' for the last line. There would be no joke! This kind of thing can happen very easily, and it leads me to my second Golden Rule, which is **PRACTISE TELLING YOUR JOKES BEFORE TRYING THEM OUT ON AN**

AUDIENCE. You may find some jokes much easier to tell than others, and if so, concentrate on these, as the chances are you will 'deliver' them better if you find them easy to relate. Similarly, if you read a joke that you like but you find it awkward to say, rephrase it slightly to suit yourself – as long as you don't lose the point of it.

An equally important Rule is **NEVER TELL A JOKE THAT WILL HURT ANYONE'S FEELINGS.** For example, it would be very cruel to tell this joke:

What happened when the budgie was run over by the lawnmower?
Shredded tweet!

to someone whose pet bird had just died. Or to tell a joke about people with big noses to someone who had a big nose. So do consider your audience carefully before you speak.

Similarly, if you know that certain subjects are guaranteed to bring a giggle to certain people, then tell jokes about those subjects. If your friends have a particularly bad-tempered form teacher who teaches maths, for example, tell lots of jokes about maths teachers, especially jokes in which the teacher comes off badly.

CHOOSE THE RIGHT MOMENT TO TELL JOKES. This is all part of 'timing', mentioned in Chapter 1. If the audience isn't in the right mood, or if their attention is distracted by something else, then it will be very hard to make them laugh. So wait until you are sure you have their attention, and they are sitting on the edges of their seats waiting for you, and *then* start your joke.

This is the moment when your nerve may fail you and you may hesitate. *Don't.* Try and get that feeling conquered at the practice stage – the rehearsal, if you like. If, when facing your audience, you still feel overcome with confusion then you haven't practised long enough. For my fifth Golden Rule is **SPEAK CLEARLY, DON'T RUSH, AND LOOK AT YOUR AUDIENCE WHEN TELLING A JOKE.** If you are a desperately shy person you perhaps ought to give up the idea of show business!

DON'T EVER TELL A JOKE TO THE SAME AUDIENCE TWICE. They are bound to remember it and will probably groan loudly.

If you are serious about wanting to make people laugh, you will always carry a notebook and a pencil with which to make a note of funny things you hear and see, but you should also note down people's reactions to jokes and funny situations to see what makes them laugh. If you go to see a funny film at the cinema, or are watching television, look at the audience from time to time to see what they find funny. They may not be the same things that you instinctively find funny, so try and find the humour in it. You want to be able to amuse everybody!

My seventh and last Golden Rule is **ONLY TELL JOKES THAT YOU FIND FUNNY.** Despite what I said in the last paragraph, if you really don't find a joke amusing then you are unlikely to be able to tell it effectively. And that wouldn't do, would it?

Once you have mastered these basic rules you can think about building up an act. It's a good idea to consider using a particular gimmick that people will associate with you, as many successful comedians do. This could be something connected with your appearance, like a funny hat or a false beard, or something you carry – like Ken Dodd's tickling stick – or it could be a catchphrase. Lots of comedians use catchphrases, and the curious thing about them is although they may not be particularly funny in themselves, they make everybody laugh, as they remind the audience of the funny people who say them.

Here are some examples to show what I mean. Do you know who said them all? The answers are given at the back of the book.

1. 'Shut that door.'
2. 'It's the way I tell 'em.'
3. 'Nick-nick.'
4. 'Greetings, Ratfans.'
5. 'Fan, dabi, dozi.'
6. 'Rock on, Tommy.'
7. 'How tickled I ham.'
8. 'Come on down, the price is right.'
9. 'Ooh! I could crush a grape.'
10. 'Boom, boom!'

You may find, if you ask your friends, that you already have a phrase you say frequently that you could develop into a catchphrase. Lots of people do. When I was at school there was one boy who was always noticing strange smells about the place, and became known for saying, 'There's a funny smell around here!' This would have been a very good catchphrase if he had been trying to make people laugh, as he could have looked his audience up and down, wrinkled up his nose, and said, in a comic fashion, 'Phew! What a funny smell!' And they would all have laughed.

With experience you will find you start to develop little routines of your own, almost without being aware of it. This is as it should be, and means that you are well on the way to becoming a successful comedian.

The most important thing of all is that you should find it fun. For enjoyment is infectious, and if you are having a whale of a time the chances are that your audience will too. Happy joke-cracking!

3 Knock on the Door

No one knows who invented the knock, knock joke but it has been around for over thirty years and is as popular today as it was in the 1950s. The first knock, knock jokes were fairly simple, like these:

Knock, knock.
Who's there?
Eileen.
Eileen who?
Eileen Dover.

Knock, knock.
Who's there?
Alec.
Alec who?
Alec Trician.

Knock, knock jokes are, of course, based on puns. They take an ordinary first name and, by changing its meaning, though not its sound, turn it into a phrase or sentence. It is the *unexpectedness* of the phrase or sentence that makes the joke funny.

As time went by, the jokes became cleverer and more complicated:

Knock, knock.
Who's there?
Anna.
Anna who?
Anna Notherthing, open the door.

Knock, knock.
Who's there?
Stan.
Stan who?
Stan Back I'm going to sneeze.

Nowadays there seems to be no stopping the knock, knock joke from becoming ever more elaborate. Look at this one:

Knock, knock.
Who's there?
M. I. B. it's a big horse.
M. I. B. it's a big horse who?
M. I. B. it's a big horse I'm a Londoner.

If you've never heard the song 'Maybe It's Because I'm a Londoner' you won't think much of the joke, but if you do know the song you will find it very clever. (It is, of course, said or sung in a London accent, hence 'M. I. B.' for 'maybe'.) Here is another fiendishly clever one that you will only appreciate if you speak French!

Frappe, frappe.
Qui est là?
Don.
Don qui?
Ee-aw, ee-aw, ee-aw!

Here are twenty-five typical knock, knocks that are particular favourites of mine. I hope they will inspire you to invent some original knock, knock jokes of your own. Start with a name and say it over and over again to yourself to see if it reminds you of anything. If, after a while, it hasn't sparked anything off, then try again with a different name. It shouldn't take long and, who knows, your efforts may be even better than these!

Knock, knock.
Who's there?
Alex.
Alex who?
Alex Plain later.

Knock, knock.
Who's there?
Arfer.
Arfer who?
Arfer Got.

Knock, knock.
Who's there?
Nana.
Nana who?
Nana your business.

Knock, knock.
Who's there?
Sultan.
Sultan who?
Sultan Pepper.

Knock, knock.
Who's there?
Homer.
Homer who?
Homer Gain!

Knock, knock.
Who's there?
Ewan.
Ewan who?
Just me.

Knock, knock.
Who's there?
Juno.
Juno who?
I dunno, Juno?

Knock, knock.
Who's there?
Doris.
Doris who?
Doris jammed again.

Knock, knock.
Who's there?
Willy.
Willy who?
Willy or won't he?

Knock, knock.
Who's there?
Emma.
Emma who?
Emma Chisit to let me in?

Knock, knock.
Who's there?
Justin.
Justin who?
Justin Time for tea.

Knock, knock.
Who's there?
Sonia.
Sonia who?
Sonia shoe, I can smell it from here.

Knock, knock.
Who's there?
Olga.
Olga who?
Olga home if you don't open up.

Knock, knock.
Who's there?
Les.
Les who?
Les go and play cricket.

Knock, knock.
Who's there?
Ivan.
Ivan who?
Ivan you pair of jeans.

Knock, knock.
Who's there?
Watson.
Watson who?
Watson your mind?

Knock, knock.
Who's there?
Ida.
Ida who?
Ida nice friend before I met you.

Knock, knock.
Who's there?
Michael.
Michael who?
Mike'll go away if you don't let him in.

Knock, knock.
Who's there?
Dwayne.
Dwayne who?
Dwayne the bath, I'm dwowning.

Knock, knock.
Who's there?
Dinah.
Dinah who?
Dinah Saur a big animal.

Knock, knock.
Who's there?
Buddha.
Buddha who?
Buddha this bun for me, would you?

Knock, knock.
Who's there?
Harriet.
Harriet who?
Harriet all my sandwiches.

Knock, knock.
Who's there?
Rosa.
Rosa who?
Rosa cabbages in my garden.

Knock, knock.
Who's there?
Gladys.
Gladys who?
Gladys Friday today.

Knock, knock.
Who's there?
Hacienda.
Hacienda who?
Hacienda knock, knock jokes.

4 Slips of the Tongue

Humour can be intentional, as when you deliberately make up a joke involving a pun, or it can be accidental. And mistakes, as we all know, are often very funny. It is human nature to laugh at other people's mistakes, and provided you can laugh at your own mistakes, too, it doesn't matter very much, but you must remember to try not to hurt people's feelings by your laughter.

In this chapter we look at verbal mistakes, and one of the most famous forms of these is called the malapropism.

Malapropisms

These verbal banana skins were named after a character in an eighteenth-century play by Richard Brinsley Sheridan. In the play (which was written when Sheridan was only twenty-three) Mrs Malaprop kept using very long words, but the trouble was that she got them muddled up and misapplied them. She would say of someone, for example, that he was 'as headstrong as an allegory on the banks of the Nile', when what she meant was as headstrong as an *alligator*. Here are some more of her famous sayings:

'Illiterate him, I say, from your memory.' (She meant *obliterate*.)
'He is the very pine-apple of politeness.' (She meant *pinnacle*.)

'It gives me the hydrostatics to such a degree.' (She meant *hysterics*.)

And here are some modern malapropisms, some of which come from real school work. You would never make mistakes like these, would you?

King Solomon had a thousand wives and a lot of conquered turbines. (*Conquered turbines* should be 'concubines'.)

Henry VIII disillusioned the monasteries. (*Disillusioned* should be 'dissolved'. Henry VIII's act was known as the 'Dissolution of the Monasteries'.)

All the French stood to attention while the band played the Mayonnaise. (*Mayonnaise* should be 'Marseillaise'.)

Beau Brummel was a well-dressed dandy from Birmingham. (. . . *from Birmingham* is wrong and is based on the fact that Birmingham is known as 'Brum'.)

A ruminating animal is one that chews its cubs. (*Cubs* should be 'cud'.)

A glass porch on a house where plants are grown is called a conservative. (*Conservative* should be 'conservatory'.)

My doctor says my eyes need testing so he's sending me to an optimist. (*Optimist* should be 'oculist' or 'optician'.)

My dad communicates daily on the train to work. (*Communicates* should be 'commutes'.)

If you take your humour seriously you will always have a notebook to hand to jot down any amusing mistakes you hear. If you have a good enough collection you may be able to write your own book on humour one day. And reading through it will give you ideas for inventing amusing mistakes of your own. See how many you can think of now, before reading the rest of the chapter.

Spoonerisms

Spoonerisms are amusing slips of the tongue in which the initial letters of key words in a sentence are transposed. They, too, were named after a person, but this time a real live one, the Reverend W. A. Spooner, who lived from 1844 to 1930 and was Warden of New College, Oxford. One morning, while announcing the next hymn, he is supposed to have said, 'Kinquering congs their titles take', and from this wonderful mistake arose a reputation for transposing the letters of words. Here are some of the sayings attributed to the Reverend Spooner:

'I have in my breast a half-warmed fish.'

'You have hissed all my mystery lectures.'

'I have frost a very dear lend.'

'He will leave on the next town drain.'

'You have tasted two whole worms.'

'Give me a well-boiled icicle.'

Here is one that he should have said. Try it out next time you go to the theatre or the cinema!

'I do apologize but I'm afraid I was sewn into this sheet.'

See if you can make up some Spoonerisms of your own. Start by thinking of an ordinary saying or phrase, and then transpose the initial letters of the most important words. 'Is this the Brighton train?', for example, might come out as, 'Is this the tighten brain?' and confuse everybody utterly!

Everyday slips of the tongue

These are the kinds of mistakes we all make – though some of us do it more often than others. Only last week I heard myself say to my son, as he took his third apple from the bowl, 'Apples don't grow on trees, you know.' He gave me a strange look and solemnly tapped his forehead. Since then he and I have collected some good slips of the tongue, and here they are for your amusement.

If you don't come back, I shan't let you go again.

They still use inches to measure horses' hands.

Today doctors can save the lives of little babies who formerly used to die from sheer ignorance.

If my grandfather were alive he'd turn over in his grave.

In a word – I don't think so.

Your head looks just like my sister's behind.

My auntie lived to be a centurion.

Keep quiet when you're speaking to me!

If the baby doesn't like cold milk, boil it.

His car was a red, X-registration hunchback.

Moths eat hardly nothing, except holes.

Faith is believing what you know to be untrue.

I went and fried the bacon in my nightdress.

Anyone who goes to a psychiatrist ought to have his head examined.

If the circumstances were on the other foot . . .

Boil the baby while I change the kettle, will you?

5 Popular Pachyderms

What on earth is a pachyderm? Before you either go scuttling for your dictionary or give up in despair, I'll explain that it is a thick-skinned quadruped – in other words, an animal such as a rhinoceros or an elephant. Now you know why it is a heading in this book!

When you think about them, elephant jokes are quite ridiculous. So why are they so funny and so popular? I think there are two main reasons. The first is precisely because they *are* so ridiculous, because they are based on the absurd. And the second is because of the nature of the elephant itself – its great size and curious trunk, together with its gentle and patient nature, make it a very lovable animal. The word-picture conjured up by the elephant joke is so illogical, and its subject is so endearing, that we laugh.

And we have been laughing at elephant jokes for a good number of years. Here are some of the earliest:

Why do elephants paint their toenails red?
So they can hide in cherry trees.
I've never seen an elephant in a cherry tree.
It shows it's a good disguise, doesn't it?

Why is an elephant large, grey and wrinkled?
Because if it were small, red and juicy it would be a strawberry.

What did Tarzan say when he saw the elephants coming?
'Here come the elephants.'

What's the difference between an elephant and a postbox?
I don't know.
Well, I shan't send *you* to post my letters.

What did Tarzan say when he saw the elephants coming with sunglasses on?
Nothing, he didn't recognize them.

How do you get four elephants in a Mini?
Two in the front and two in the back.

How do you get four hippopotamuses in a Mini?
You can't, it's full of elephants.

Over the years elephant jokes have acquired the status of classics. Here are some that I consider to be classic examples:

Where does a two-ton elephant sleep?
Anywhere it wants to.

What do you get if you cross an elephant with a mouse?
Massive holes in the skirting board.

How can you tell if an elephant's been sleeping in your bed?
By the peanut shells.

How can you tell if there's an elephant in your oven?
You can't shut the door.

How can you tell if an elephant's been in your fridge?
By the footprints in the butter.

What's the difference between a biscuit and an elephant?
You can't dip an elephant in your tea.

What did the river say when the elephant sat in it?
Well, I'm dammed.

What do you have to know to teach an elephant tricks?
More than the elephant.

Why can't two elephants go swimming at the same time?
They only have one pair of trunks.

What do you give a seasick elephant?
Lots of room.

What time is it when an elephant sits on your car?
Time to get a new car.

What do you give a nervous elephant?
Trunkquillizers.

How can you tell a monster from an elephant?
A monster never remembers.

Gradually elephant jokes have developed into slightly different forms. Here are some of the newest. The first three are developments of the very earliest:

How does an elephant get into a cherry tree?
Sits on a stone and waits till it grows.

How does an elephant get out of a cherry tree?
Waits till autumn and floats down on a leaf.

What's grey and white and red all over?
An embarrassed elephant.

Why did the elephants leave the circus?
They were tired of working for peanuts.

How do you get down off an elephant?
You don't, you get down off a duck.

Why do elephants have big ears?
They're hoping Noddy will pay the ransom.

Why do elephants have wrinkled ankles?
They lace their shoes too tightly.

How do you hire an elephant?
Lift it up on to the table.

How do you scold an elephant?
Say, 'Tusk, tusk.'

What would you do with a blue elephant?
Try to cheer it up.

> A team of elephants was playing football with a team of fleas. Fred Flea was just about to score a goal when Edna Elephant, defending, squashed him flat. The referee blew his whistle. 'You've killed him, I shall have to send you off.'
> 'But I only meant to trip him up,' said Edna sadly.

This last joke is of quite a different type to the usual two-liner. It might lead you to try out some elephant jokes of your own. It also brings in a different type of animal, as does this one:

What's worse than a giraffe with a sore throat?
An elephant with a blocked nose.

And here is yet another way in which the elephant joke has developed. The idea is the same, and the joke is based on a pun:

How do you get two whales in a Volkswagen?
Over the Severn Bridge.

How many more can you think up?

6 April Fool!

The first of April is traditionally the day on which we play practical jokes, or April Fools, on our friends. The joke can be a simple one, such as calling out to your brother at breakfast time, 'Hey, you forgot to put your trousers on this morning!' and when he looks down to check, saying, 'April Fool!' loudly. Or it can be a much more elaborate trick needing careful preparation, like those described later in the chapter. Whatever the trick, it has to be played before twelve noon, or the joke is said to be on the person who played it and he makes an April Fool of himself.

In France an April Fool is called a *poisson d'avril* (literally, 'April fish') and in Scotland they call someone who has been made a fool of on 1 April a *gowk* ('cuckoo').

No one knows for certain why this day has become the day for playing practical jokes, but there are a number of theories. One is that it is the feast day of Lud, a Celtic god of fun and good humour who was once worshipped by the Irish and the Welsh. Another is that it is a relic of Cerealia, the Roman festival in honour of Ceres, the corn goddess, which was celebrated in April. The story goes that when Ceres' daughter, Proserpina, was carried off to the underworld by Pluto, Ceres heard the echoes of her scream and tried to find her by seeking the place from which the voice had come, but the search proved to be a fool's errand, for she was seeking the echo, not the voice. Yet another theory is that the day commemorates that on which Jesus was sent to and fro between the high priests Annas and Caiaphas, and from Pontius Pilate to Herod.

Whatever the truth of its origin, most of us enjoy playing jokes on our family and friends on 1 April. But did you know that sensible and serious organizations like the B.B.C. and our national newspapers often let their hair down on this day too? One famous occasion on which this happened was in 1957, when the B.B.C. television news programme *Panorama* showed a report on the Italian spaghetti harvest. The film showed women carefully pulling long strands of spaghetti off trees and filling baskets with them, and the programme was presented by a highly respected broadcaster, the late Richard Dimbleby. Now most people know that spaghetti is made from a wheat dough rolled into strands, but because the programme was presented in such a serious manner, large numbers of viewers took it seriously, forgetting the day on which it was shown.

Another wonderful April Fool joke was played by the *Guardian* newspaper in 1977. They printed a whole supplement about two islands called San Serriffe, set somewhere in a tropical ocean. These islands had a military ruler called General Pica, and their capital city was called Bodoni. Anyone who knows anything about printing is aware that all these names are printing terms, but the joke was so painstakingly carried out – the newspaper wrote about the islands' economy, tourism, politics, and so on – that many readers were completely fooled and the paper received several requests for further information about the islands from would-be tourists.

Most of us, however, are not able to play jokes on such a grand scale. For those who just want to tease their family and friends, here are a few suggestions.

Morning paper

This is a good joke to play on your parents if they have a morning newspaper delivered. Save a copy of the newspaper from a few days before and then, on the morning of 1 April, go downstairs before the rest of the family is up and swap the outside pages of the new newspaper with those of the old one, so that you have a newspaper whose front page says 1 April but whose inside pages are several days old! Stick the paper back in the letterbox and wait out of sight until someone gets up and starts to read the paper. It may be a while before they realize what has happened, but when they start looking puzzled and turning the pages back and forwards, be on hand to shout 'April Fool!' (Be sure to give them the correct pages of the newspaper afterwards or you may get yourself into real trouble!)

Big black spider joke 1

Spiders are harmless creatures but no one seems to like them much, do they? Try walking into the classroom at

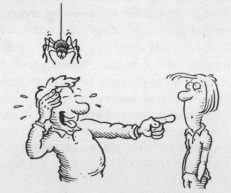

school, or into a room at home where your family or friends are, and saying, 'Aaaaggghhh! Help! There's an *ennnooorrmous* spider over there!' Everyone in the room will look towards where you are pointing, and some may squeak in horror. As soon as they look and see there is nothing there, shout, 'April Fool!'

Big black spider joke 2

This joke needs a little more preparation. See if you can get hold of some pipe cleaners. Paint four of them (or colour them with a felt-tip pen) black, and twist them round each other to make the spider's eight legs. Where they meet in the centre will form its body. Then leave it in a corner of the room, or suspend it from a length of invisible thread from a lampshade or the curtains. As soon as someone notices it, be ready to shout, 'April Fool!'

Problem drawers

The preparation for this trick will have to be done the night before. It is a good one to play on someone who is always late in the morning and scrabbling about for their clothes.

Take out the drawer of a chest of drawers where your victim keeps his or her clothes. Remove all the clothes from the drawer and hide them in a safe place, then turn the drawer upside down and replace it in the chest. When your victim goes to the drawer in the morning to find their clean clothes they will be mystified as to what has happened. You could stick a little 'April Fool' notice on the drawer to explain.

Cottoning on

This one is a good trick to play on your mother. You will need to wear a jacket or coat, and have a reel of thread to match the jacket, and a needle.

Thread the needle without cutting the thread off, and push it through the jacket from the inside to the outside. Remove the needle from the thread and put it away in a safe place, and leave a few centimetres of the thread showing. Put the reel of thread in an inside pocket.

Just before you leave the house on the morning of 1 April, make sure your mother sees the thread. She is sure to try and remove it for you, thinking it is a loose thread from your jacket, but, of course, as she pulls it more and more thread will keep unravelling! Say, 'April Fool!' before she starts to get cross!

The final straw

This trick is a good one to play at break time at school. You will need to do a small amount of preparation the day before, and you will need a drinking straw and a pin.

Make two holes about 5 cm from each end of the straw by pushing the pin right through it. The straw is then ready for use. When you want to play the joke, put the straw in a bottle of pop and drink from it, covering up the holes at the top of the straw with your fingers. Offer a friend a sip of the drink. They, of course, will not know about the holes in the straw, and will eagerly try and drink through it – but nothing will happen! Unless the holes at the top of the straw are covered it will be impossible to draw any liquid up the straw. Call your poor friend an April Fool and then let them have a drink of the pop without the straw. You needn't tell them how you did the trick!

7 Ridiculous Riddles

Nowadays riddles are often used as a way of presenting a joke, usually one based on the pun. But they used to be genuinely enigmatic puzzles, and date back to times of antiquity. In Greek mythology the Sphinx, a fabulous monster, posed the question: 'Which animal walks on four feet in the morning, on two feet at midday, and on three feet in the evening?' and devoured anyone unable to answer it. Can you guess what the answer is? It is man, who, in infancy (the 'morning' of life) crawls on all fours, in adulthood walks on two feet, and in old age walks on three – the third 'foot' being the stick with which he aids his walking.

In the last century the poet Christina Rossetti posed this riddle:

> There is one that has a head without an eye,
> And there's one that has an eye without a head:
> You may find the answer if you try;
> And when all is said,
> Half the answer hangs upon a thread.

Do you know what the answer is? It is a pin and a needle.

Other poets wrote riddles in verse. See if you can solve these two:

> In marble halls as white as milk
> Lined with a skin as soft as silk,
> Within a fountain crystal clear
> A golden apple doth appear.

No doors are there to this stronghold
Yet thieves break in and steal the gold.

In spring I look gay
Decked in comely array,
In summer more clothing I wear;
When colder it grows
I fling off my clothes,
And in winter quite naked appear.

The answer to the first is an egg; to the second is a tree.
  There are also riddles based on numbers. For example:

What odd number, when beheaded, becomes even?

How can you halve eight and end up with nothing?

The answer to the first is 7, i.e. $EVEN; to the second is $\frac{0}{0} - 0 = 0$. As you can see, an element of trickery has started to appear! See if you can answer these number riddles:

If it takes four minutes to boil one egg how long does it take to boil three eggs?
Four minutes!

49

What is bigger when it's upside down?
The number six (6).

Why is the number ten like the number eleven?
*Because twice ten is twenty and twice eleven is twenty-two
(twenty too).*

If you dug a hole 120 cm wide, 100 cm long and 75 cm
deep, how much earth would be in it?
None, of course!

What yard has four feet in it?
One containing a dog.

   This last riddle looks as if it is a number riddle at first,
but in fact it is really a word riddle, because it is based on a
pun. Here are some more word riddles:

How can you make an opera singer out of two five-pound
notes?
Because two five-pound notes equal one tenner (tenor).

What's the longest word in the English language?
Smiles – because it has a mile between the first and last letters.

What is the smallest room?
The mushroom.

What is the largest room?
The room for improvement.

How can you make notes out of stone?
Rearrange the letters.

What comes at the end of every year?
The letter R.

Why did the owl 'owl?
Because the woodpecker would peck 'er.

The last of these riddles is becoming more of a joke than a riddle.

The next ten riddles are also jokes, and they are all based on animals:

What do you call high-rise flats for pigs?
Styscrapers.

What has six legs, four ears and a tail?
A man on a horse.

Why do cows wear bells?
Because their horns don't work.

What do you get if you cross a hedgehog with a giraffe?
A ten-foot toothbrush.

What do porcupines eat with their cheese?
Prickled onions.

Why is it hard to talk in front of a goat?
It always butts in.

Why did the ant elope?
Nobody gnu.

What is a caterpillar?
A worm with a sweater on.

Why did the lobster blush?
Because it saw the salad dressing.

Here are ten of my own favourite joke riddles:

How do you start a rice pudding race?
Sago.

If a buttercup is yellow, what colour is a hiccup?
Burple.

What would you call two bananas?
A pair of slippers.

When is a chair like a piece of material?
When it is satin.

What do you call a camel with three humps?
Humphrey.

What nationality is Santa Claus?
North Polish.

What do the letters C. I. D. stand for?
Coppers in disguise.

How do people dance in Saudi Arabia?
Sheikh to sheikh.

What was the name of the engineer's wife?
Bridget.

A final thought on riddles to test your wits. There is a new kind of riddle going around in which you are given the answer but have to provide the question. For example, what was the question to this answer?

'Pleased to meet you, Dr Presume.'

If you can work out the answer to that, see if you can work out some back-to-front riddles of your own!

'Dr Livingstone, I presume?'

8 'There's a Fly in My Soup!'

Next to elephant jokes, waiter jokes must be the best loved. The classic waiter joke started with:

'Waiter, waiter, there's a fly in my soup!'

to which there were a number of classic responses:

'Don't speak so loud, sir, everyone will want one.'

'It's all right, sir, it can swim.'

'Don't worry, sir, the spider on the roll will catch it.'

'I'm sorry, sir, I didn't know you wished to dine alone.'

and so on.

One of the most brilliant visual interpretations of the

waiter joke appeared in Mel Brooks's film *Silent Movie*. Two men are sitting eating at a table outside a restaurant; the camera cuts to a shot of a pest-control van careering along, its advertising symbol being an enormous model fly sitting on the roof of the cab. The scenes are cut from one shot to the other, and the viewer knows what will happen, but not when or how, thus building up a good amount of tension. Sure enough, eventually the van collides with another vehicle, the fly is released from its moorings and sails through the air, to land in the diners' soup. The fly is so big it covers the entire table, and this ridiculous ending to the joke that has been building up for some time leads to hysterical laughter on the part of the audience.

Why did the waiter joke ever come into being? One of the things we joke about is the familiar and accessible. We like to joke about things that are part of the safe and familiar surroundings of our lives, and food is central to this aspect of them. We all know that it is necessary to sustain life, but it is much more than that. It is part of our social fabric, it gives us a warm, contented and secure feeling, and if it tastes good, it is a delicious treat. And so we make jokes about it, out of our affection for it. The waiter aspect of the joke is just a means of expression. It brings in the comic elements of the irate male customer (it is never a woman, possibly because women complain less), the incompetent waiter and the terrible food and/or service – British catering being generally known for its low standards.

The original 'fly in the soup' joke developed a few variations, as follows:

'Waiter, what's this fly doing in my soup?'
The breast-stroke, sir.

'Waiter, what is this soup?'
'It's bean soup, sir'.
'I don't care what it's been, what is it now?'

'Waiter, waiter, what's this in my soup?'
'I've no idea, sir, all insects look the same to me.'

'Waiter, waiter, there's no turtle in this turtle soup.'
'No, and there aren't any shepherds in the shepherd's pie either.'

'Waiter, waiter, there's a flea in my soup.'
'Shall I tell him to hop it, sir?'

'Waiter, waiter, there's a fly in my soup.'
'Throw it a Polo mint as a lifebelt, sir.'

Nowadays waiter jokes come in all kinds of forms. There are even some that start with the waiter speaking:

'How did you find your steak, sir?'
'With a magnifying glass.'

'We have practically everything on the menu, sir.'
'So I see. Will you bring me a clean one, please?'

'What will you have to follow the roast chicken, sir?'
'Indigestion, I expect.'

Here are some favourites old and new that work their way through the menu:

'Waiter, waiter, this plate is wet.'
'That's the soup, sir.'

'Waiter, waiter, I'm in a hurry. Will my omelette be long?'
'No, sir, round, like everybody else's.'

'Waiter, waiter, do they ever change the tablecloths in this establishment?'
'I don't know, sir, I've only worked here for a year.'

'Waiter, bring me a burnt sausage, a pile of greasy chips and a leathery egg.'
'Oh, I couldn't possibly serve you food like that, sir.'
'Why not? You did yesterday.'

'Waiter, have you smoked salmon?'
'No, but I used to smoke a pipe, sir.'

'Waiter, waiter, there's a button in my salad.'
'It must have fallen off while the salad was dressing.'

'Waiter, waiter, do you serve crabs?'
'Sit down, sir, we serve anybody.'

'Waiter, waiter, you've got your thumb on my steak.'
'I don't want it to fall on the floor again, sir.'

'There's only one piece of meat on my plate, waiter.'
'Hang on, sir, and I'll cut it in two.'

'Waiter, waiter, have you any wild duck?'
'No, sir, but I can annoy a tame one for you.'

'Waiter, waiter, why is my steak and kidney pie all mashed up?'
'You said, ''Fetch me steak and kidney pie and step on it,'' sir.'

'Waiter, waiter, I have a complaint.'
'This is a restaurant, sir, not a hospital.'

'Waiter, waiter, I can't eat this dreadful food. Call the manager.'
'It's no use, sir, he won't eat it either.'

'Waiter, waiter, there's soap in this food.'
'That's to wash it down with, sir.'

'Waiter, waiter, this lemonade is all cloudy.'
'It's all right, sir, it's just the glass that is dirty.'

'Waiter, waiter, this coffee tastes like mud.'
'Well, sir, it was ground only a few minutes ago.'

'Waiter, a cup of coffee without cream, please.'
'I'm sorry, sir, we're out of cream. Will you have it without milk?'

'Waiter, waiter, what is this stuff, coffee or tea?'
'What do you mean, sir?'
'It tastes like paraffin.'
'Well, if it tastes like paraffin it must be tea, the coffee tastes like paint-stripper.'

9 The Scrawl of the Wild

Graffiti is a difficult subject to write about in a children's book. We all know that writing messages on walls is wrong and that only badly behaved people do it, but some graffiti (and it is a very small proportion) may be witty and amusing enough to make you stop and think, or to make you laugh. And if it does these things, then we have to admit that it is good as a joke. (In fact, the graffiti in these pages are probably wittier and more amusing than any you are likely to see sprayed on a wall.)

The word 'graffiti' comes from the Italian word *graffio* meaning 'a scratch', for the original graffiti were scratched, not written or sprayed, on walls. It is a very ancient form of defacement. If you are ever lucky enough to visit Pompeii or Herculaneum in Italy, those famous Roman cities that were engulfed by a volcanic eruption in A.D. 69, you will see that the Romans wrote graffiti. They scratched the equivalent of 'Kilroy was here' and other, ruder, messages in Latin on the city walls.

'Kilroy was here' is the sentence everyone thinks of when they think of graffiti. Who was Kilroy and why does he pop up in so many places? James J. Kilroy was an inspector of tanks and warships being constructed during the Second World War at the Bethlehem Steel Company's Quincy shipyard in Halifax, Massachusetts, U.S.A. To show his employers that he was indeed inspecting their products, he scribbled in yellow crayon 'Kilroy was here' on everything he examined. Soon these words began to appear in all kinds of unrelated places, and it is believed that the 14,000 or so shipyard workers who subsequently entered the armed services were responsible for spreading the message to all corners of the world.

It is particularly unusual because nearly all graffiti are anonymous, apart from the 'Sue loves Simon' variety.

I don't think that anyone should write on walls, but you can have a lot of fun in your own room by fixing large sheets of blank paper to the walls and creating original and amusing comments. You could invite all your friends to have a go and see who writes the most amusing message. What makes graffiti amusing? Well, it is the neat way in which a witticism is expressed. Graffiti tend to be divided into two forms – the original one-line message, and the message formed when someone has added a second line to an existing statement. Let's look at the one-liners first. One of the most popular, which could be seen around almost everywhere a few years ago was ––––––– rules, O.K. It began as a football fan's battle cry – Arsenal rules, O.K.? – and became a cult. Look at some of these developments:

Queen Elizabeth
Rules U.K.

QUEEN ELIZABETH RULES U.K.

QUEENSBURY RULES K.O. (The Marquess of Queensberry formulated the rules under which boxing is carried out, and a K.O. is a knock-out in boxing terms.)

ROGET'S THESAURUS RULES O.K., ALL RIGHT, CERTAINLY, DOUBTLESS, YOU BET (*Roget's Thesaurus* is a reference book that gives alternative words that mean the same.)

AMNESIA RULES . . . ER . . . UM . . . (Amnesia is a condition in which people forget things.)

You will probably be able to think of some more. What about these one-liners? They should make you stop and think:

THE M25 ISN'T ALL IT'S CRACKED UP TO BE (The new M25 is already suffering from cracks in its surface.)

JUST THINK: TOMORROW TODAY WILL BE YESTERDAY

RICHARD COEUR DE LION – FIRST HEART TRANSPLANT (*Coeur de lion* is French for 'lion heart'.)

FOR THE MILLIONTH TIME – STOP EXAGGERATING

IF YOU CAN'T READ WATCH THIS SPACE

NOSTALGIA ISN'T WHAT IT USED TO BE

Or what about these? They are strictly for culture vultures:

THE VENUS DE MILO IS PERFECTLY ARMLESS
(The Venus de Milo is a famous statue without any arms.)

TURNER PAINTED HIS SKIES BY NIMBUS ('Nimbus' is a kind of cloud and Turner was famous for his landscapes showing large amounts of cloudy sky. It is, of course, a pun on 'painting by numbers'.)

BEETHOVEN WAS SO DEAF HE THOUGHT HE WAS A PAINTER

VAN GOGH WAS EAR (This famous artist cut off his ear.)

TOLKIEN IS HOBBIT FORMING (J. R. R. Tolkien is famous as the author of *The Hobbit*.)

MR KIPLING DOES WRITE EXCEEDINGLY GOOD BOOKS

WAS HAMLET PIGLET'S SON?

A lot of graffiti, however, are amusing because they consist of a first line written by one person, to which a second line has been added by another. The first line might be part of a poster or advertising slogan, like this:

HARWICH FOR THE CONTINENT

to which some wit has added:

BOURNEMOUTH FOR THE INCONTINENT

The joke, of course, is a pun on the word 'continent', and the reason the graffito (singular of graffiti) is funny is because the second person thought of the word with an entirely different meaning. What about these:

THINK!
OR THWIM

EUREKA!
YOU DON'T SMELL TOO GOOD YOURSELF

THIS IS THE AGE OF THE TRAIN
OURS WAS 106

KEEP BRITAIN TIDY
POST YOUR RUBBISH ABROAD

I'VE LIVED ON EARTH ALL MY LIFE
I'D RATHER EAT FOOD

I LOVE TEACHER
FRIED OR BOILED?

Finally, here are some very silly graffiti, which I hope will make you laugh and inspire you to create some for yourself (but *only* in your notebook or on sheets of paper pinned to the wall with your parents' permission):

YESTERDAY I COULDN'T SPELL EDUCATED, NOW I ARE IT

BETWEEN YOUR EYES IS SOMETHING THAT SMELLS

PASSENGERS ARE REQUESTED NOT TO CROSS THE LINES
IT TAKES HOURS TO UNTANGLE THEM

I LOVE GRILS
DON'T YOU MEAN GIRLS?
WHAT'S WRONG WITH US GRILS?

GOBLIN YOUR FOOD IS BAD FOR YOUR ELF

BAD SPELLERS OF THE WORLD UNTIE

AN APPLE A DAY KEEPS THE DOCTOR AWAY
AN ONION A DAY KEEPS EVERYONE AWAY

CAN I HAVE A DATE?
HOW ABOUT 1066?

BREAKFAST IN LONDON – LUNCH IN NEW YORK
LUGGAGE IN HONG KONG!

SNOOPY HAS FLEAS

I HATE GRAFFITI
I HATE ALL ITALIAN FOOD

I QUOTED THIS WALL IN MY EXAM – AND PASSED

10 People Who Live in Grass Houses

The title of this chapter may have set you guessing, but before I go any further I will reveal that it is part of the punch-line to a well-known shaggy dog story (see below). For those who are still puzzled, a shaggy dog story is one of those long, rambling jokes whose point is difficult to spot – exactly like a large, hairy dog whose eyes and nose are hidden by his coat. You must have heard one at some time, for certain people seem very fond of them, and will pounce on you when you are alone and spend the next ten minutes relating one. By the time they get to the end, you will have forgotten what the beginning was!

When I was at school I used to think that shaggy dog stories had been invented to make those who told them unpopular. For no matter how long and rambling the

story, or how absurd the ending, the listeners to those that I tried to tell would always groan loudly and walk away, and for the next few days avoid me if I showed the slightest sign of saying, 'Did I ever tell you the one about . . .?'

Shaggy dog stories can really be divided into two types, though the results of telling both types are similar. The types are: those that end with a pun, and those that end with a damp squib, i.e. an ending that is very weak indeed. It is the very weakest of these endings that makes the jokes amusing to those who like them, and infuriating to those who don't. I have collected ten of my favourites, of which only two are puns. Here they are:

An African tribe found a beautiful golden throne in the jungle. They carried it home to their village, where everyone marvelled at it. The head man ordered that it should be put in a special hut, guarded night and day, and that no one should be allowed into the hut. And so it was done.

No sooner was this accomplished than the rainy season began. Day after day the rain poured down, for two whole months. At the end of this time the headman decided he must go and have a peep at his golden throne. He tiptoed into the hut, followed by his wife, and was horrified when he discovered that the throne was covered in green mould, from the damp in the hut. 'It just goes to show, darling,' said his wife, 'that people who live in grass houses shouldn't stow thrones.'

On an island in a tropical sea lived a fisherman. Every morning he went out in his boat to catch as many fish as he could, and each evening when he returned, no matter how many wonderful fish he had caught, nor how big they were, he would tell his family of the amazing monster-sized fish he had seen and almost caught.

The fisherman had two sons. One was called Towards, and the other was called Away, and eventually the day dawned when his sons were big enough to go out fishing with him for the first time. When he returned that evening he was more excited than ever.

'Nellie,' he said to his wife, 'you wouldn't believe the huge fish we saw today. It was ten feet long, and it came up to the boat, reached up over the side and grabbed Towards and swallowed him whole!'

'Oh dear,' said Nellie. 'How terrible! Oh, poor, dear Towards!'

'But I'm afraid that's only half the story,' said the fisherman, shaking his head. 'You should have seen the one that got Away.'

Well, I did warn you about shaggy dog stories! The rest of those in this chapter are of the damp squib variety, because I think the book as a whole has quite enough puns in it! But the pun types are perhaps the easier to construct yourself, as all you need to do is to think of a well-known saying and then reconstruct it and build a story round it. See if you can build a shaggy dog story round the saying 'There's no fool like an old fool'.

Meanwhile, here are my favourite damp squibs:

A group of cowboys were sitting round a camp fire telling stories. One of them, a tall, dark-haired fellow called Hank, said, 'I know an Indian chief who never forgets anything. The devil can have my soul if I'm not telling the truth.'

That night the devil appeared and asked Hank to take him to the Indian, as he didn't believe him.

'I'll show you,' said Hank. 'Come with me.'

For three days and nights they travelled, and finally they approached the Indian's camp. Hank introduced the devil. 'Do you like eggs?' the devil asked.

'Yes,' replied the Indian.

Hank and the devil went away, and twenty years later Hank died. The devil went off to find the Indian, anxious to claim Hank's soul.

'How!' said the devil, greeting the Indian.

'Fried,' replied the Indian.

A family of tortoises went into a café for some ice-cream. Father ordered vanilla ice-cream, Mother ordered strawberry, and young Timmy Tortoise ordered chocolate. They were just about to start eating their ice-creams when Father said, 'I

think it's going to rain. Would you pop home, please, Timmy, and fetch my umbrella?'

Off went Timmy. Three days later he still hadn't returned. 'I think,' said Mother Tortoise to Father Tortoise, 'that we had better eat Timmy's ice-cream before it melts.'

A voice from the door called out, 'If you do that I won't go!'

Gabriel and Thomas, the oldest inhabitants of Wittering Parva, were one day persuaded to take a train to the big city, to visit some of their relatives. Neither of them had ever left the village before. Because it was a long journey, and the train had no buffet car, a friend gave them a bunch of bananas to eat on the way. They had never eaten bananas before, either.

They travelled along for a while, marvelling at the speed, and then began to feel a bit peckish. 'Try one of these bananas,' said Gabriel to Thomas.

'I don't mind if I do,' said Thomas to Gabriel.

Just as Thomas took a bite of his banana, the train went into a tunnel. 'Have you eaten your banana yet?' wailed Thomas.

'No,' said Gabriel.

'Well, don't touch it,' said Thomas. 'I took one bite and went blind.'

One autumn evening Bill and Will went out collecting conkers. They collected a huge bag, and decided to go and share them out in the graveyard. Just as they went in, two conkers rolled out of the bag. 'We'll get those later,' said Bill, 'let's go and share out the others first.'

As they were sharing them out a little girl walked across the graveyard taking a short cut home, for it was getting dark. To her horror she heard voices, 'One for you, one for me, one for you . . .' She flew to the gate in a terrible state and bumped straight into a policeman.

'What's the matter, little girl?' he asked, for she was trembling with fear.

'Oh,' she said, 'there are ghosts in the graveyard and they're sharing out the dead bodies. Listen.' They both stood still, and a voice floated out to them on the night air, 'One for you, one for me, and we mustn't forget those two by the gate.'

Naughty young Dennis had been tearing round the house and garden all morning, creating havoc and getting under his mother's feet. Her patience had begun to wear thin. The last straw came when he ripped his trousers climbing a tree.

'Take those trousers off and go upstairs and read a book till lunchtime,' she said. 'I'll mend the trousers then and you can put them on again. But I don't want to see or hear you until one o'clock.'

Half an hour later Dennis's mother heard a noise coming from the cellar. 'You naughty boy,' she cried, 'are you running about down there with no trousers on?'

'No, madam,' a man's voice replied. 'I'm reading the gas meter.'

One hot sunny day a hippopotamus strolled into a café and ordered a large orange juice with ice. The waiter was amazed to see the hippo and to hear him speak but served him with the glass of orange juice. The hippo drained the orange juice and sucked the ice-cubes, then silently handed the waiter a five-pound note. The waiter, thinking that the hippo would know nothing about money, decided to cheat him and handed him one pound in change. 'I hope you enjoyed the orange juice,' he said. 'It's not often we get hippos in here, you know.'

'With orange juice at four pounds a glass, I'm not surprised,' replied the hippo.

The SS *Luxuriana* was spending the summer taking people on luxury cruises round the Mediterranean. The ship had wonderfully comfortable cabins, a first-rate menu, and dances and cabaret shows every evening. Among the performers was a very clever magician, who could make things disappear, produce rabbits out of hats, and so on.

One of the sailors on the ship had a parrot, which took a great dislike to the magician. Every time he performed his act the parrot would shout, 'Phoney, phoney!'

The last cruise ended in disaster, for the ship sank and all that remained was one plank of wood with the parrot sitting on one end of it and the magician sitting on the other. The parrot sighed deeply, turned to the magician, and said, 'O.K., clever clogs, what did you do with the ship?'

And finally, the ultimate shaggy dog story. Or should it be a shaggy horse story?

A man went to an auction sale to buy a horse. He found a beautiful animal, which seemed just what he wanted, but it was very cheap. 'Is there anything wrong with this horse?' he asked the dealer who was selling it. 'It's a low price for such a good-looking animal.'

'There's just one small thing,' said the dealer. 'He likes to sit down on bananas. Whenever he sees one he goes and sits on it, and refuses to move.'

'He's not likely to see many bananas where I live,' said the man. 'I think I'll buy him.'

So he paid for the horse, got on it, and set off for

home. On the way they had to ford a stream. Right in the very middle, the horse sat down and the man slid off. 'There must be a banana in this stream,' thought the man. So he waded around in the water, looking all round the horse, but could see nothing that resembled a banana. He pulled at the horse's bridle, and urged it on, but it just sat there and refused to move.

After a while the man gave up. He climbed out of the stream, and, wet through and extremely angry, made his way back to the auction to find the dealer who had sold him the horse.

'Oi,' he shouted. 'That horse you sold me. You said the only thing wrong with it was that it sat on bananas. But it sat down right in the middle of a stream where there were no bananas and I've tried everything and I can't get it to move!'

'Oh dear,' said the dealer. 'I forgot to tell you. It sits on fish too.'

11 Adding Insult to Injury

Humour can sometimes be rather unkind. We know we shouldn't laugh when someone slips on a banana skin and falls over, or if someone else's trousers fall down, but we do, because it is a natural reaction. Being amused at someone else's discomfort, even if we manage to restrain the actual laughter, seems to be instinctive. It is because one of the functions of humour is to make us feel safe, and if we feel safe and secure when someone else isn't, we laugh. We are relieved that it is they and not us who have got themselves into a pickle. One of the funniest memories from my childhood dates from my early schooldays, when we were taken on a nature ramble by a short, plump teacher. We had to go through the kind of stile that consists of two tall upright stones set close together, and she got stuck in the middle. Redder and redder in the face, she struggled to free herself, and we all collapsed with mirth. We tried to control ourselves because we knew we were being very rude, but we couldn't, it was such a funny sight.

Another type of unkind humour is the wisecrack – the short, barbed retort that is usually being nasty about somebody. As long as we don't take these remarks seriously – or mean them seriously – they can be very funny, but you should never make a wisecrack about someone who is unfortunate in any way because it would be very cruel.

Wisecracks can be simple, one-line jokes addressed to the person you are with and either about them or about a third party, or they can be two-line jokes (or longer) like any other kind except that they are distinguished by the fact that they are being insulting about somebody. For example, you might say to someone (and it had better be a good friend!):

Don't look out of the window. People will think it's Hallowe'en.

in which case you are implying that they are so ugly their face looks like a mask. Or you might say of someone else:

She has long red hair all down her back. Pity it doesn't grow on her head.

Or you might simply tell a joke:

'Is that perfume I smell?'
'It is, and you do!'

The very best wisecracks are said on the spur of the moment in response to something someone says or does, and because of this it is almost impossible to explain how to make them. But I have included below some of those that I like in the hope that they may inspire you to create some of your own when the moment strikes.

'Where do you bathe?'
'In the spring.'
'I said where, not when.'

The last time I saw a face like yours I threw it a fish.

'That suit fits you like a glove.'
'I'm glad you like it.'
'I don't. It sticks out in five places.'

'A funny thing happened to my mother in Glasgow.'
'Oh, really? I thought you were born in Liverpool.'

JULIET: You remind me of the sea.
ROMEO: *Why? Because I'm so wild and romantic?*
JULIET: No, because you make me sick.

'Our dog is just like one of the family.'
'Really? Who?'

I never forget a face, but in your case I'll make an exception.

POMPOUS LADY: I suppose you call that monstrosity a work of art.
ANTIQUES SALESMAN: *No, madam, it's a mirror.*

'Is the actress good looking?'
'Well, I wouldn't say she's ugly but she's got a perfect face for radio.'

'Whenever I'm down in the dumps I buy myself a new dress.'
'Oh, so that's where you find them!'

'How could I ever leave you?'
'By bus, train, car, plane . . .'

'I must go now. Don't trouble to see me to the door.'
'It's no trouble. It will be a pleasure.'

'I've just come back from the beauty parlour.'
'Pity it was closed.'

'Your tights are all wrinkled.'
'But I'm not wearing any.'

My brother is built upside down. His nose runs and his feet smell.

'You remind me of my favourite boxer.'
'Muhammad Ali?'
'No, he's called Fido.'

12 Hilarious Howlers

In Chapter 4 we looked at verbal howlers – slips of the tongue. In this chapter we are going to consider the written kind – misprints, misused words, terrible translations and other mistakes which unintentionally cause great amusement in their readers.

Newspaper headlines

The trouble with writing a headline for a newspaper is that you only have a small space in which to fit enough words to tell the readers what the story is all about. This has resulted in some classic bloomers:

MONTY FLIES BACK TO FRONT

QUEEN TO BE SOLD BIT BY BIT

WELSH PUBLIC BODIES GET CIRCULAR

NEW POLLUTION THREAT AS MINISTER HEADS FOR BEACHES

PASSENGERS HIT BY CANCELLED TRAINS

PRICES RISE – BUT GROCERS SAY THEY WILL NOT HIT HOUSEWIVES

MAN RECOVERING AFTER FATAL CRASH

MAN CRITICAL AFTER LORRY RUNS HIM DOWN

POLICE FOUND SAFE UNDER BLANKET

MAGISTRATES ACT TO KEEP THEATRE OPEN

Sometimes newspapers just produce printing errors, called 'literals', and these, too, make very funny reading:

POP STAR FOUND DAD IN BATH

OFFICER CONVICTED OF ACCEPTING BRIDE

WEATHER FORECAST: A DEPRESSION WILL MOPE SLOWLY ACROSS ENGLAND

TOURISTS HEAD FOR SIN AND SEA

BLACKROCK TO HAVE PARENT–TEACHER ASSASSINATION

Crazy advertisements

Of course, newspapers don't just carry funny headlines. Some of them make the most wonderful blunders in their advertisements:

WANTED: Sensible young woman to wash, iron and milk two cows.

FOR SALE: Piano to suit beginner with legs.

FOR SALE: Semi-det. hse., 3 beds, lounge, din. room, kit., bath, sep. W.C. 5 miles Hastings.

REQUIRED: Lady for 6 hours' work per week to clean small officers.

WIDOWS made to order. Send for details.

FOR SALE: One collapsible baby. Good condition.

1933 Rolls-Royce hearse for sale. Original body.

SECRETARY requires work at home. Anything awful considered.

GRANDAD, 1980, 2-litre. 40,000 miles only. Good condition.

YOUNG WOMAN wants washing and cleaning three days a week.

SMALL FLAT available mid-August. Suit two business ladies. Use of communal kitchen or two gentlemen.

UPRIGHT piano for sale, reasonably priced. Owner is getting grand.

SAVE time and cut fingers with our new mincing machine.

FURNISHED flat to let. Two rooms, k. and b., £300 per calendar month. Electricity and rats included.

FOR SALE, 20 miles Birmingham. Lovely little gentleman's weekend cottage.

WORTHING. Comfortable apartments to let, 5 mins. sea. Germs moderate.

WANTED – wet fish or experienced man or woman to run business.

MATTRESSES repaired, pillows cleaned, new ticks supplied at reasonable prices.

PRECAST concrete foreman required.

FOAM rubber cushions for sale at rock bottom prices.

YOUNG MAN requires comfortable bed-sitting room with boar.

WANTED: Two young apprentices to live in. Will be treated as one of the family.

As well as newspapers and other publications, signs of all kinds can be a great source of amusement. It always seems to me that the people who write signs have absolutely no sense of humour, or they wouldn't produce examples like these:

In a country lane
When this sign is under water the road is closed to traffic.

On a village green
It is forbidden to throw stones at this notice.

In a park in Ohio, U.S.A.
These seats are for the use of ladies. Gentlemen should sit on them only after the former are seated.

At the edge of a lake
Any person passing beyond this notice will be drowned. By order of the magistrates.

Outside a school
Dead slow children crossing.

At a railway station
Toilets out of order. Please use platforms 5 and 6.

On Southend Pier
DON'T THROW
PEOPLE BELOW

At the roadside
Caution. Men at work. Dead slow.

Outside a church hall
In this hall, Sunday at 6 p.m.
THE DEVIL

On an electricity pylon
Danger! Touching these wires will result in instant death.
Anyone found doing so will be prosecuted.

Outside an Indian restaurant
Delicious and authentic curries. One visit is enough to
make you regular.

In an office kitchen
Staff should empty teapots and then stand upside down
on the draining board.

Outside a workshop
Installers of central heating and plumbing for 14 years
    A. C. Puddle & Co Ltd

In a department store
Bargain basement upstairs.

On a chemist's shop
We dispense with accuracy.

In a dry cleaner's
Customers leaving garments more than 30 days will be
disposed of.

In shop windows
Ears pierced while you wait.

Why shop elsewhere and be cheated when you can come
here?

Girls ready to wear clothes.

John Smith butchers pigs like his father.

Terrible translations

Anyone who has ever travelled abroad, or even read the instructions printed on foreign packaging, will have encountered the often hilariously funny efforts that people make to translate their language into English. These can involve genuine mix-ups or mis-spellings of words, so that a menu may start with the appetizing-sounding 'Soap of the day', or just ignorance of the way words are used in English. One result of the latter, which I treasure, is a guidebook entitled *How to Visit the Beauties of Florence*. Of course, the English, who are renowned for their inability to speak foreign languages, never hear about the howlers that they make. I heard of one lady who spent two weeks in Greece greeting everyone with the word 'squid' (*kalamari*) instead of 'good morning' (*kalimera*)!

Translating words from one language to another and then back to the original highlights the way misunderstandings can arise. In a recent example, 'out of sight, out of mind' was translated into Russian, and then back into English. It ended up as 'invisible lunatic'!

Here are some classic terrible translations to make you laugh. Next time you go abroad, see if you can find some good ones of your own and write them down in your notebook. Let's start with some more of those menus:

Hand and egg
Frightened eegs
Sauceage eeg an chaps
Coughee Eggspress

Speciality of the hows:
Young Dear Hunter
(flush of young dear, muchrooms, objerjeans, in white whine sorts, all cooked up in your seat)

Fizz Soup
Boled eegs in creme sorse
Muscles of Marines
Frog leagues

Lioness cutlet
Tongue leaf with leaves
Surprised chicken
Rice hashed

Marooned Duchess with steak surprise
Two peasants
Larks in the spit
Angry duck in orange sorts

Now for some notices to guests, taken from hotels all round the world:

In case of fire alarm the hall porter.

In the event of fire, the visitor, avoiding panic, is to walk down the corridor and warm the chambermaid.

After the typhoid epidemic guests are assured that all vegetables are boiled in water passed by the manager.

If you are satisfactory, tell all your friend.
If you are unsatisfactory, warn the waitress.

Sports jackets may be worn, but never trousers.

By a hotel swimming pool in Spain:
Bathers are reminded that they must be fully dressed on entry into the swimming pools and fully dressed on leaving the swimming pools.

In a French café:
Persons are requested not to occupy seats in this café if they do not wish to consume them.

And finally some random notices and advertisements, finishing up with one of those wonderful foreign food packet instructions:

From a French newspaper:
'Le capitaine Miller, en uniforme des Cold Cream Guards.'

Advertisement in a Portuguese newspaper:
'Engliss shorthanded typist. Efficien. Useless. Apply otherwise.'

Advertisement for a Nigerian bus company:
'The comfort in our buses is next to none.'

Driving instructions from Germany:
'At a police-controlled crossing, drivers wishing to turn right should wait for the all-clear before running over the policeman.'

On a foreign food packet:
'To do what: besmear a backing pan, previously buttered with a good tomato sauce and after, dispose canelloni, lightly distanced between them in a only couch.'

13 Ireland Strikes Back

I spent a long time wondering whether to include Irish jokes in this book. The problem was that they are very popular in Britain, but obviously it is also wrong to make fun of people just because they are Irish. But in the end I decided to include this chapter because it gives me a chance to explain that Irish jokes aren't necessarily about the Irish, they are about any group of people who are considered less knowledgeable and sophisticated than ourselves.

As we saw in the previous chapter, one of the functions of humour is to make us feel safe and secure. A function which is an extension of this is to make us feel secure in our own superiority over people we consider lesser beings because they are not so worldly and well educated as ourselves. Explained in these terms the Irish joke sounds very unpleasant indeed, and if it is taken seriously it is both unpleasant and offensive. Fortunately most British people, when they tell an Irish joke, have no such motive in mind, they are just relating a funny story.

All countries have their version of the Irish joke. In Britain we call it that because when the starving Irish peasants came in great numbers to this country in the last century, they were uneducated and ignorant of many of our more sophisticated ways. But the Irish themselves have Irish jokes. A Dubliner, for example, will tell jokes about the people of Kerry and Cork – rural areas where the inhabitants tend to be a bit behind the times. In Italy they tell jokes about the peasants who live in the poor south, in France they joke about the Belgians eating chips all the time, in America they make jokes about the Polish immigrants. It's a kind of one-upmanship, possibly also tinged with fear that we who are clever and wise and live a comfortable life might become poor, ignorant peasants if our lives were to change.

Included in this chapter are some classic Irish jokes. But they are Irish jokes with a difference, for not once will you see the words 'Irish', 'Ireland', 'Mick', 'Paddy' or any other identifying labels. They have been replaced by blanks, so you can fill them in with whatever you like. You can turn them into jokes about another country or about Mars and the Martians, if you like. I think you will find that they are just as funny – and I will have proved my point about Irish jokes not necessarily being about the Irish!

—————— wanted to keep an accurate record of his son's height. So every six months he stood him up against a wall and made a mark on his head.

How to tell if a —————— cake is cooked: make two cakes, one large and one small, and put them in the oven. When the small one is burnt the large one is done.

Did you hear about the wealthy —————— who advertised for a daily woman and hired all 365 of them?

Mrs —————— made her living-room curtains 10 cm too short but she solved the problem by cutting 10 cm off the top and sewing it on to the bottom.

Did you hear about the —————— family who lived in the ground-floor flat of a high-rise block? They were stuck indoors for a week when the lift broke down.

—————— ice-cream melts in the fridge, not in your mouth.

——————: How many A-levels have you got?
——————: *Three, Maths and Advanced Maths.*

BOSS: You said you were ill yesterday but you were seen at the football match.
EMPLOYEE: *Oh, no, sir, that was someone who looked just like me. I told him so myself at half time.*

When —————— started his new job as a dustman he lifted off the lid of the first bin and exclaimed, 'Somebody's filled it up already!'

A —————— cricket match was once abandoned because both teams turned up wearing white.

FIRST MAN: Excuse me, but can you tell me where the other side of the road is?
SECOND MAN: *It's over there.*
FIRST MAN: That's funny. When I was over there they said it was over here.

–––––– is really smart. He can tell the difference between a real seven-pound note and a forged one.

'Am I the only man you've ever kissed?'
'Indeed you are, but not the best-looking.'

How do you make a –––––– laugh on Boxing Day?
Tell him a joke on Christmas Eve.

14 'There Was a Young Lady . . .'

You will recognize the heading of this chapter as one of the most popular first lines of that most popular form of funny verse, the limerick. Limericks are verses of five lines, the third and fourth of which are usually half the length of the first, second and fifth, and which conform to a regular pattern of scansion, or rhythm. The first limericks appeared in books published in the 1820s, but it was that most celebrated limerick writer, Edward Lear, who made them really popular after the publication of his *Book of Nonsense* in 1846. Lear, who lived from 1812 to 1888, was primarily an artist, and he was employed by the Earl of Derby to illustrate a book about the latter's private zoo. While Lear was staying with Lord Derby he wrote nonsense rhymes to amuse his patron's grandchildren, and it was these poems that formed the basis of the *Book of Nonsense*.

Lear's limericks usually repeated part of the first line in the last:

> There was an old man of Dumbree,
> Who taught little owls to drink tea;
> For he said, 'To eat mice
> Is not proper or nice,'
> That amiable man of Dumbree.

There was a Young Lady whose chin
Resembled the point of a pin;
So she had it made sharp,
And purchased a harp,
And played several tunes with her chin.

But as the limerick developed this custom was dropped,
and the verses' endings became wittier:

A girl of great beauty, named Jane,
While walking was caught in the rain.
She ran – almost flew,
Her complexion did too,
And she reached home exceedingly plain.

Then someone had the bright idea of constructing the last words of lines from words that sounded the same but which should have been spelt differently – though they weren't. This gave rise to some very amusing limericks:

There was a young lady of Twickenham
Whose boots were too tight to walk quickenham.
She bore them awhile,
But at last, at a stile,
She took them both off and was sickenham.

A lady there was from Antigua
Who remarked to her spouse, 'What a pigua!'
He retorted, 'My Queen,
Is it manners you mean
Or do you refer to my figua?'

A girl who weighed many an oz
Used language I dare not pronoz
When a fellow, unkind,
Pulled her chair out behind,
Just to see, so he said, if she'd boz.

See if you can construct a limerick or two for yourself. The rhythm should be as set out below, where / stands for a stressed syllable and ˘ for an unstressed one, but don't worry if you don't get it quite right to start with:

There wăs ă grĕat chíef ŏf thĕ Sióux
Who ĭntŏ ă gún barrĕl bliŏux
Tŏ sĕe ĭf 'twăs loădĕd;
Thĕ ríflĕ explódĕd
Aš hĕ shŏuld hăve knŏwn ĭt wŏuld dióux!

Here are some first lines for you to try:

A charming young lady named Pat

A cheerful young Cockney from Bow

A squirrel who lived in a tree

A brave young explorer on Mars

But of course not all funny verse comes in the form of a limerick. I once wrote the shortest poem in the history of English literature, and I like to think it is funny:

> Ode to a Goldfish
> O
> Wet
> Pet!

Verse of all kinds can be funny. One of the most amusing kinds is that which is a parody of another well-known rhyme, that is, it mimics it. Take the nursery rhyme:

> Mary had a little lamb
> Its fleece was white as snow
> And everywhere that Mary went
> The lamb was sure to go.

There are several versions of this poem:

> Mary had a little lamb,
> Its fleece was black as soot,
> And into Mary's bread and jam
> Its sooty foot it put.

> Mary had a little lamb –
> You've heard this tale before.
> But did you know she passed her plate
> And had a little more?

> Mary had a little lamb,
> She ate it with mint sauce,
> And everywhere that Mary went
> The lamb went too, of course.

> Mary had a little watch
> She swallowed it one day,
> And now she's taking Beecham's pills
> To pass the time away.

> Mary had a parrot.
> She killed it in a rage.
> For every time her boyfriend came
> The darned thing told her age.

Here are some parodies of Christmas carols:

> While shepherds watched their turnip tops
> All boiling in the pot,
> A lump of soot came rolling down
> And spoilt the blooming lot.

> Good King Wenceslas looked out
> On the Feast of Stephen;
> A snowball hit him on the snout
> And made it all uneven.
> Brightly shone his conk that night
> Though the pain was cruel,
> Till a doctor came in sight
> Riding on a mu-oo-el.

Again, parodies are quite simple to make up for yourself.

To finish the chapter, here is a selection of funny verse of all kinds, which I hope may give you some ideas for constructing rhymes of your own:

> My bishop's eyes I've never seen
> Though the light in them may shine;
> For when he prays he closes his,
> And when he preaches, mine.

> Twinkle, twinkle, little star,
> I don't wonder what you are.
> You're the cooling down of gases
> Forming into solid masses.

> Latin is a language
> As dead as dead can be.
> First it killed the Romans
> And now it's killing me.

Algy met a bear,
The bear met Algy.
The bear was bulgy,
The bulge was Algy.

Little Willie;
Pair of skates;
Hole in the ice;
Pearly Gates.

And if you have difficulty trying to write in verse, don't despair. Remember:

Don't worry if your life's a joke
And your successes few;
Remember that the mighty oak
Was once a nut like you!

15 Batty Books

'Batty books' is the title I have given to those jokes where the names of the book and the author fit together because the author's name is a pun. (If you've forgotten what a pun is see page 9.) I was very fond of batty book jokes when I was a child – which shows that they have been around for quite a long time – and one of the earliest ones I can remember is *Over The Cliff* by Eileen Dover.

Since then people have become more inventive about batty book jokes, and have created some amazing names. What about *Snacks For All* by T. N. Bickies? Batty books are one of the easiest kinds of jokes to make up yourself, and the way to do it is to think up the author's name first and then invent a title they might have written. What book do you suppose Robin Banks would have written, for example? Or what about Dan D. Lyon, or Rick O'Shea?

For your amusement and inspiration, I have collected together my especial favourites. Here they are:

Carpet Fitting by Walter Wall
Better Gardening by Anita Lawn
Tilling The Soil by Rosa Cabbages
Home Shopping by May Lauder
German Cars by Otto Mobilesz
Tightrope Walking by Betty Falls
The Plumber's Handbook by Lee King
Off to Market by Tobias A. Pigg
Modern Science by Alec Tricity

Hair Care by Dan Druff
Happy Holidays by Heidi High
Rush Hour Travel by Stan Dinroomonly
Luxury Travel by Ira Carr
On Vacation by Holly Day
Chemistry Class by Tess Tubes
Travel to the Pole by Anne Tarctic
Kittens Galore! by Claude Sofa
What the Future Holds by Claire Voyant
Wearing Hats by Sonia Head
Closing Time by Les Avvenother
Is it Love? by Fred Itisnt
Legal Practice by Sue Andwin
Festive Fare by Mary Christmas
Who Killed Cock Robin? by Howard I. Know
Feeding Dogs by Norah Bone
Selling Fish by Hal E. Butt
My Dear Watson by L. M. N. Tree
Investigating Ghosts by Denise R. Knocking
Visiting the Dentist by Hugo First

16 Medical Mirth

If we are afraid of something, or if we find it distasteful or upsetting, we often make a joke about it to hide our fear. This is partly to fool others, because we don't want to appear to be afraid in their presence, and partly to fool ourselves, because we don't want to admit, even to ourselves, that we are afraid. It's all part of 'putting on a good face' – trying to appear in control of a situation which makes us feel insecure and unhappy. And I think this is the reason that 'doctor, doctor' jokes were first thought of and also why they have become so popular.

Most of us dislike going to the doctor because we associate it with feeling ill, having to stay in bed, taking nasty medicines and probably not being allowed to eat our usual food. And so we make a joke about it, to try and fool ourselves into thinking that we don't mind at all, that it is as much fun as going to see a friend.

Doctor jokes are characterized by the patient being nervous and worried about some extraordinary condition and by the doctor being unfeeling and heartless, as in these examples:

'Doctor, doctor, I keep thinking I'm a pair of curtains.'
'Pull yourself together.'

'Doctor, doctor, this ointment you gave me makes my leg smart.'
'Try rubbing some on your head, then.'

'Doctor, doctor, I keep thinking I'm a dustbin.'
'Don't talk rubbish.'

'Doctor, doctor, my wife is a kleptomaniac.'
'Is she taking anything for it?'

'Doctor, doctor, I have this urge to cover myself in gold paint.'
'You're suffering from a gilt complex.'

'Doctor, doctor, I feel like a pound note.'
'Go shopping, the change will do you good.'

'Doctor, doctor, I can't get to sleep at night.'
'Lie on the edge of the bed and you'll soon drop off.'

'Doctor, doctor, I feel like a spoon.'
'Sit down and don't stir.'

'Doctor, doctor, can you cure my running nose?'
'I'll give you a tap on it.'

'Doctor, doctor, I feel like a pack of cards.'
'Wait over there, I'll deal with you later.'

'Doctor, doctor, I've swallowed the film out of my camera.'
'Let's hope nothing develops.'

All the examples above are based on puns, but there are others of the heartless doctor variety that do not depend on puns at all:

'Doctor, doctor, I'm so unhappy. Nobody ever notices me.'
'Next.'

'Doctor, doctor, my son has just swallowed a ballpoint pen.'
'I'll be right over.'
'What should I do until you arrive?'
'Use a pencil.'

'Doctor, doctor, if I take these pills will I get better?'
'Well, no one has ever come back for more.'

'Doctor, doctor, I'm having difficulty breathing.'
'I'll soon stop that.'

'Doctor, doctor, how long have I got to live?'
'Well, if I were you I shouldn't start reading any serials.'

'Doctor, doctor, I feel dizzy for half an hour after I get up every morning.'
'Try getting up half an hour earlier.'

'Doctor, doctor, I keep thinking I'm invisible.'
'Who said that?'

'Doctor, doctor, I keep putting on weight in certain places. What should I do?'
'Stay out of those places.'

There are even a few jokes in which the doctor speaks first:

'How are you feeling after your heart operation?'
'I seem to hear two heartbeats.'
'I wondered what had happened to my watch.'

'You need glasses.'
'How can you tell?'
'I could tell as soon as you walked through the window.'

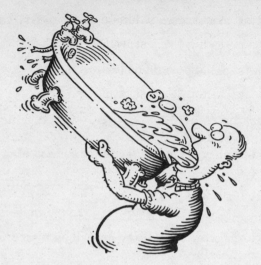

'Did you drink your medicine after your bath?'
'After drinking the bath I didn't have room for the medicine.'

'Have your eyes ever been checked?'
'No, they've always been blue.'

'How did you get that splinter in your finger?'
'I scratched my head.'

'I'm terribly sorry to have to tell you this, Mrs Sidebottom, but you have rabies.'
'Quick, give me a piece of paper!'
'What for, to write your will?'
'No, to write a list of people I want to bite!'

Jokes in which the doctor speaks first tend to conform less to type than do the other doctor jokes, and many of them are rather silly, but no less funny for that. See if you can make up some doctor jokes. Here are some first lines to start you off:

'Doctor, doctor, I keep thinking I'm a goat.'

'Doctor, doctor, I've just swallowed a sheep.'

'Doctor, doctor, everyone thinks I'm a cricket ball.'

'Doctor, doctor, I've just swallowed a bar of soap.'

17 X Certificate

'X certificate' was the classification which used to be given to films to which the under-sixteens were not admitted. The term came to be used to describe anything that wasn't quite proper, and that is why it is the heading for this chapter. For the jokes within it aren't quite proper, either – they are jokes about forbidden territory.

A lot of humour is based on making the unacceptable acceptable, as we have already seen. The jokes about doctors, for example, by making us laugh about illnesses and doctors' visits, make them acceptable to us. And the jokes about X-certificate subjects work in a similar way, which is why some people don't like them.

Most young people, however, delight in jokes about subjects that aren't quite proper, so I had to include a chapter about them in the *Joke Box*. I'm going to start with sick jokes – those nasty ones about violence that would be truly horrific if we were to take them seriously. There is a whole collection of American jokes of this kind, called the Little Willie jokes and the Little Audrey jokes. You may have come across some of them:

When Little Willie pushed his sister down the well his mother was very vexed. 'We'll have to buy a filter now,' she said angrily.

Little Audrey was with her grandmother watching the roadmenders outside the house. Her grandmother saw a coin in the road. 'There's a silver dollar,' she shouted, and ran to pick it up, but a steamroller squashed her flat. And Little Audrey laughed and laughed, because she'd known all along that it wasn't a silver dollar but a dime.

In Britain the equivalent of these jokes are those about the wicked mother:

'Mummy, I don't want to go to America.'
'Shut up and keep swimming.'

'Mummy, I've missed Daddy.'
'Then take another shot at him.'

'Mummy, all the kids say I look like a werewolf.'
'Shut up and comb your face.'

'Mummy, what is a vampire?'
'Shut up and drink your soup before it clots.'

'Mummy, why can't we have a waste disposal unit?'
'Shut up and keep chewing.'

'Mummy, what's for dinner?'
'Shut up and get back in the oven.'

And not even the fathers can be trusted:

FIRST MAN: I've cured my son of biting his nails.
SECOND MAN: *How?*
FIRST MAN: I chopped his fingers off.

There are lots of other sick jokes that don't fall into any particular category except that they are nasty. So don't read the next couple of pages unless you have a strong stomach:

BARBER: Were you wearing a red scarf when you came in?

CUSTOMER: *No.*

BARBER: Oh dear, I must have cut your throat.

What do you get if you cross the Atlantic with the *Titanic*?
Half-way.

CIRCUS CLOWN: What was the name of that man who used to put his arm down the lion's throat?

TRAPEZE ARTIST: *I don't know, but they call him Lefty now.*

FIRST MAGICIAN: What happened to the lady you used to saw in half?

SECOND MAGICIAN: *She's living in London and Edinburgh.*

What's a skeleton?
Bones with people scraped off.

What do you get if you mow over a budgie?
Shredded tweet.

'Why don't you go out and play football with your brother?'
'*I'm tired of kicking him around.*'

What kind of boats do vampires like?
Blood vessels.

What goes ho ho ho plop?
Santa Claus laughing his head off.

What were Batman and Robin called after they'd been run over by a steam roller?
Flatman and Ribbon.

'What were your dying husband's last words?'
'"I don't see how they can make a profit selling this ham at 10p a tin."'

What is black, floats on water and shouts 'Knickers!'?
Crude oil.

What is black, floats on water and shouts 'Underwear!'?
Refined oil.

No, the two jokes above are not sick jokes, but an introduction to the other kind of X-certificate joke, the vulgar variety. These are the jokes that are a bit rude – the kind you wouldn't want your prim relatives to hear, the kind that answer this question:

What is a sick joke?
Something you mustn't bring up in polite conversation!

Here are ten of them. Be careful whom you tell them to!

What did the toothpaste say to the toothbrush?
'Squeeze my bottom and I'll meet you outside the tube.'

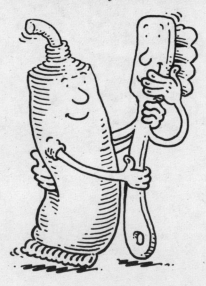

Who is short, uses bad language, and is afraid of wolves?
Little Rude Riding Hood.

When does a bee fly with its back legs crossed?
When it's looking for a B.P. station.

Why did the sand blush?
Because the seaweed.

How do you keep the kitchen free of flies?
Put a bucket of manure in the dining-room.

SARAH: (*writing*)   Roses are red, violets are blue . . .
JEN: (*giggling*)   *And mine are white!*

What's green, round and smells?
Kermit's bottom.

MR HIGGINS: I've just bought a pig.
MRS BIGGINS: *Where will you keep it?*
MR HIGGINS: In my bedroom.
MRS BIGGINS: *But what about the smell?*
MR HIGGINS: It'll just have to get used to it.

MARY: What do you clean your top teeth with?
JOHN: *A toothbrush.*
MARY: What do you clean your bottom with?
JOHN: *The same.*
MARY: Do you? I use paper!

Which rude saint is Santa Claus named after?
Saint Knickerless.

18 The Last Word

This chapter is called 'The Last Word' not because it is the end of the book but because it is about epitaphs – those inscriptions that either are or are intended to be, carved on tombstones. Epitaphs fall into three categories. There are those that have been genuinely carved on headstones and are unintentionally funny; those that have been deliberately written in a satirical manner and were never intended to be actually used on graves; and many that are apocryphal – that is, no one knows whether they are genuine or not, but they make very amusing reading.

In the modern world death has become a taboo subject, but in years gone by, when it was much more a part of life than it is nowadays, it was something people joked about. The following would be considered very bad taste nowadays if they were to be written after someone's demise:

Epitaph for Charles II

Here lies our Sovereign Lord, the King,
Whose word no man relies on,
Who never said a foolish thing,
Nor ever did a wise one.

John Wilmot, Earl of Rochester

Here lies my wife:
Here let her lie!
Now she's at rest,
And so am I.
John Dryden (1631–1700)

This spot is the sweetest I've seen in my life
For it raises my flowers and covers my wife.

On Merideth, organist at Oxford:

Here lies one blown out of breath
Who lived a merry life, and died a Merideth.

These epitaphs were all intended to be satirical. If you read the following on tombstones you might think they were written by people with a sense of humour, too, but I fear their humour was unintentional:

Richard Kendrick was buried here
On 29th August 1785
By the desire of his wife, Margaret Kendrick.

Here lies the body of Thomas Vernon
The only surviving son of Admiral Vernon.
Died 23rd July 1753.

Here lies the body of John Mound
Who was lost at sea and never found.

This stone was erected in memory of John MacFarlane
Drowned in the waters of the Leith
By a few affectionate friends.

Jeremiah Brown, 1826–1851
This gallant young man gave up his life in an attempt to
save a perishing lady.

Nettlebed Churchyard, Oxfordshire:

Here lies father, and mother, and sister, and I:
We all died within the space of one short year.
They were all buried at Wimble except I,
And I be buried here.

And here are just a few of the apocryphal variety. I
doubt if they ever appeared on anyone's grave, but they
will amuse you and possibly help you to think of some
amusing epitaphs of your own.

Old Tom is gone (too soon, alas!)
He tried to trace escaping gas.
With lighted match he braved the fates
Which blew him to the Pearly Gates.

Here lies the mother of children seven,
Four on earth and three in heaven;
The three in heaven preferring rather
To die with mother than live with father.

Here lies a man who met his fate
Because he put on too much weight.
To overeating he was prone
But now he's gained his final stone.

Here lies the body of Michael Shay
Who died maintaining his right of way.
His case was clear and his will was strong
But he's as dead as if he were wrong.

He passed the lorry without any fuss
And he passed the cart of hay,
He tried to pass a swerving bus
And then he passed away.

Here lies our M.P. He lied all his life and he's lying still.

Underneath this pile of stones
Lies all that's left of Sally Jones.
Her name was Briggs, it was not Jones,
But Jones was used to rhyme with stones.

19 Dizzy Dictionary

One of the silliest and most enjoyable forms of jokes is that provided by what I call daft definitions – that is, definitions of what words *ought* to mean. These are almost all puns, and are based on the *sound* of the word to be defined rather than its meaning. Take the word that heads the A list – aardvark. An aardvark is an animal, and its name comes from the Afrikaans words for earth and pig. But what does it sound like in English? ' 'ard work' – so we give it a silly definition – 'something that makes you very tired'. Once you start thinking about words in this way there is no end to the number of daft definitions you can make up. You can use both English words and foreign words and phrases. What about *à la carte*? This is a French phrase you will see on menus in restaurants, and it means, literally, by the card – or ordering a meal from a range of available dishes listed on the card. But what does it mean if we give it a daft definition based on its sound? 'By wheelbarrow'!

Are you beginning to understand the idea? Here is my dizzy dictionary. If there are any words you do not know, then look up the real meaning of them in a proper dictionary. I have given you up to twelve daft definitions for each letter of the alphabet. There are many, many more. When you have read mine, try and compile one for yourself, all the way from A to Z, using different examples. Think of the word to be defined first, and say it over to yourself to see if it sounds like anything else, then give it a silly definition based on the sound. Here are some examples for you to try, but don't do so until you have read all the way through the dizzy dictionary!

Amazon, bizarre, coffin, doldrums, enclose, feline, gem, hootenanny, igloo, Juan, kidnap, lynx, maximum, niece, otter, polygon, quack doctor, ruthless, *son et lumière*, tulips, ultramarine, verse, waist, Xmas, yawn, zeal

A

aardvark: something that makes you very tired
à la carte: by wheelbarrow
aloe: a greeting
annexe: it's Anne's turn next
aperitif: a set of dentures
arbour: where boats lie at anchor
ardour: the entrance to our house
armada: feminist beginning to a prayer
aroma: gypsy wanderer
axe: what to do with a question

B

baggage: instrument for measuring bags

baize: what a hound does

bandit: something that was outlawed

barometer: instrument for measuring the contents of barrows

beadle: insect found in old churches

bison: something you wash your hands in

blubber: to whale

borough: to gain temporary use of

boycott: cradle for male babies

bruise: makes tea

C

cache: hidden money

Caesar: police order to arrest a woman

campus: collection of boy scouts in tents

canasta: tin for holding tea

catkin: feline relatives

cattle: place to keep cats, as in kennel

chimpanzee: flower monkeys like

climate: what you do with a ladder
code: having a running nose
coincide: flat surface of penny, etc

D

dandelion: big cat very fussy about its appearance
debate: lure for de fish
deceit: where to sit down
deign: person from Denmark
Delilah: inflatable air bed
diet: Welshman's food
dogma: puppy's mother
drawing-room: dentist's surgery

E

each: minor irritation
eagle: what all men are created
earwig: hairpiece with built-in hearing aid
e.g.:   what a h.e.n. lays
etching: what a dog with fleas does
eureka: exclamation, as in, 'Eureka garlic!'
explain: to parachute
eyebrow: very intellectual

F

faith: the part of a person you recognize
fete: garden party worse than death
fever: when one person helps another out
fiddlesticks: what you play a violin with
fjord: Norwegian car

flattery: living in an apartment
foible: what Aesop wrote
foolscap: hat with a D on it
fortitude: life after forty-one

G

gargoyle: treatment for a sore throat
germicide: viruses that kill themselves
gorilla: part of cooker used for making toast
gorgeous: someone who eats a lot
granary: where your mum's mother lives
grime: that which doesn't pay
groan: old enough to complain
guest: thought about it
guise: the opposite of 'dolls'

H

halo: an angel's greeting
hatless: the man who carried the world on his
    shoulders
hence: birds that lay eggs
hermit: a woman's hand
history: a man's account of what happened
humbug: an insect that doesn't know the words

I

icicle: an Eskimo's bike
icons: what pigs eat under oak trees
impale: to put in a bucket

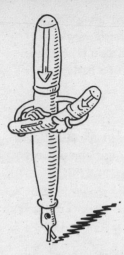

inkling: a baby pen
insecticide: suicide by a beetle

ire: opposite of 'lower'
irritation: watering the desert
intent: on a camping holiday
in toto: wearing a ballet skirt

J

jeep: an inexpensive vehicle
joking: what happens when you gag too much
Juno: have you any idea?
joust: merely

K

karma: the vehicle mother drives
kayak: confection baked for birthdays and Christmas
kernel: the nut in charge of a regiment
khaki: device that unlocks a vehicle's door
kidney: joint in a child's leg
kindred: dislike of one's relations
kinship: boat shared with the family
kipper: person who spends his time asleep
knowledge: shelf on which reference books are kept
Korea: the way you earn your living

L

lapse: what we have when we sit down
lattice: green salad vegetable
launch: midday meal at sea
ledger: someone who rents a room in a house
lemming: kind of fruit that can be made into a drink
lesson: what someone has when they are sunbathing

lice: things that give you illumination
lobster: cricketing term for a bad bowler
logarithm: lumberjacks' dance

M

malady: polite term of address for a woman
manse: belonging to a man
mayor: female horse
melancholy: unhappy sheepdog

mews: poetic cat
millennium: insect with a great number of legs
mince: sweets with holes in the middle
moose: Scottish rodent
mower: a bit extra
myth: young female moth

N

napkin: when all the family's asleep
nautical: bad behaviour in a boat
necks: the one immediately following
negligent: man's nightdress
Nicholas: not wearing underwear
nightingale: stormy evening
nom de plume: called a feather
noose: what we read in the noosepapers

O

oboe: an American tramp
octopus: a cat with eight legs
ode: a debt
offal: really bad
operetta: employee of the telephone company

P

pail: the way you look before you kick the bucket
pane: what glaziers get when they cut themselves
panther: someone who makes trousers
papal: the population of Ireland
parasite: someone who lives in Paris

pas de deux: father of twins
pauper: an American father
peace: vegetables eaten with fish and chips
phlox: a number of sheep
pitcher: what you produce in an art class

Q

quadrangle: argument in college
quiche: sign of affection

R

radish: the colour of a beetroot
ramshackle: chain used to tie up a male sheep
raven: going mad
rebate: to put another piece of cheese in the mousetrap
regulate: telling off Reg about his timekeeping
relief: what happens to trees in spring
ringleader: the first one in the bath
riot: something not made by two wrongs
robin: a thieving bird
rosette: Rose had a meal

S

sago: how to start a rice pudding race
salaam: to close the door hard
sample: that's enough
sari: an apology
sculler: student at Oxford or Cambridge
selfish: what a fishmonger does
shamrock: imitation stone

sitar: someone who looks after Indian babies
sonata: a contradiction – it isn't
spider: she was seen

T

table d'hôte: the table's on fire
taiga: large striped cat
tangent: man with a suntan
tee-hee: Chinese waiter
thaw: how a cowboy feels when he's forgotten his thaddle
toboggan: reason people attend auctions
tock: clock language
tortoise: what our teacher did
trigonometry: being married to three people at once
trowel: what a gardener dries himself on

U

udder: not this one
uninhibited: where no people live
urchin: what's under 'er mouth

V

vanilla: capital of the Philippines
Venice: Italian query, as in, 'Venice the next gondola?'
vesper: quiet way to talk in church
vice versa: rude Italian poetry
vicious: kind regards, as in, 'best vicious'

viper: snake that keeps the windscreen clean
vixen: vicar's son

W

wade: hang on for a moment
wan: pale because lonely
werewolf: kind of fur coat
wick: seven days
wind: past tense of 'win'
winsome: be lucky in a competition
winnow: part of the house you see out of
wombat: bat with which to play wom

X

Xenophon: ancient Greek telephone
X-ray: the late Raymond

Y

yashmak: what Yash wears in the rain
yarrow: place on the Tyne
yoga: dessert made from milk
yokel: an Alpine form of singing
youth: to employ for a purpose

Z

zinc: part of the kitchen fittings

20 Zoo Time

The jokes in this chapter are mostly about our four-footed friends, though a few of them concern creatures of the six- and even eight-footed varieties.

With the exception of giraffe jokes, and jokes about cross-breeding, jokes about animals do not really fall into any particular category. The fact that they are about animals is the only characteristic they have in common – otherwise they are a complete hotch-potch of puns, riddles, absurdities and general silliness, and I have arranged them by species rather than by type of joke.

But before I reveal to you the complete menagerie, I want to point out the two distinct types of animal joke that do exist: those about giraffes and those about hybrids (i.e. cross-breeds).

Giraffe jokes are similar in nature to elephant jokes. They are funny because of the absurdity both of the joke and of the animal it is about; and, like elephant jokes, have a certain cosiness because the giraffe, too, is a lovable animal. It looks to us like one of nature's freaks, but of course it is superbly suited to its environment, its long neck enabling it to browse on high branches, its dappled colouring excellent camouflage as it moves through light and shade.

Here is a selection of giraffe jokes. Do you think they are like elephant jokes?

Why does a giraffe have a long neck?
To connect its head to its body.

Why else does a giraffe have a long neck?
Because its feet smell.

If a giraffe gets wet feet, will he develop a cold in the head?
Yes, but not until next week.

Why do giraffes have small appetites?
Because a little goes a long way.

What is a giraffe's favourite joke?
A tall story.

Is a baby giraffe ever taller than its mother?
Yes, when it sits on its father's shoulders.

What do you call a giraffe that stands on your toe?
Anything you like, its head is too far away for it to hear you.

What do you get if you cross a giraffe with a dog?
An animal that barks at low-flying aircraft.

The last giraffe joke is also a 'hybrid' joke. There are lots of them and they are easy to make up yourself. They can either be based on puns or just on a combination of absurd ideas. To make some up for yourself, try writing two columns of animal and bird names and seeing if you can think of a funny result of crossing different species together. They can be as absurd as you like! Just look at these:

What do you get if you cross a bear with a kangaroo?
A fur coat with pockets.

What do you get if you cross a sheepdog with a jelly?
Colliewobbles.

What do you get if you cross a dog with a vegetable?
A Jack Brussel.

What do you get if you cross a cow with a camel?
Lumpy milkshakes.

What do you get if you cross a pig with a zebra?
Striped sausages.

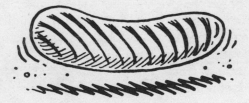

What do you get if you cross a chicken with a poodle?
Pooched eggs.

What do you get if you cross a carrier pigeon with a woodpecker?
A bird that knocks before it delivers its message.

What do you get if you cross a cat with bandages and antiseptic?
A first-aid kit.

You will, of course, have noticed that not all the animals in the above jokes are crossed with other animals. Well, it doesn't really matter what they are crossed with in this kind of joke, though it is more of a challenge if they are both animals. But it is the end result that really matters.

Now for some other animal jokes. This is the Brandreth Menagerie. It starts with the largest animals and goes down to the very smallest:

Where do you weigh whales?
At a whale-weigh station.

What do hippopotamuses have that no other animal has?
Baby hippopotamuses.

What's a crocodile's favourite game?
Snap.

What animal breaks the law?
A cheetah.

Why did the mother kangaroo scold her children?
Because they ate biscuits in bed.

'In Australia I used to chase kangaroos on horseback.'
'I didn't know kangaroos rode horses.'

What do reindeer say before they tell you a joke?
'This one will sleigh you.'

If a quadruped has four feet and a biped has two feet, what is a zebra?
A stri-ped.

Why are four-legged animals such bad dancers?
Because they have two left feet.

What do you call a pony with a sore throat?
A little hoarse.

'My horse is very polite. When he comes to a fence he stops to let me go over first.'

'Mum, do you water a horse when it's thirsty?'
'Yes, dear.'
'Good. I'm just going to milk the cat.'

What did the horse say when he got to the end of his nosebag?
'This is the last straw.'

Why wouldn't the piglets listen to their father?
Because he was such an old boar.

What do you call pigs who live together?
Pen friends.

FIRST SHEEP: Baa-aa-aa-aa.
SECOND SHEEP: *Moo.*
FIRST SHEEP: What do you mean, 'Moo'?
SECOND SHEEP: *I'm learning a foreign language.*

A goat was in a rubbish dump looking for food. It discovered a can of film and ate it. Another goat came along and asked if the can of film was any good.

'It was all right,' replied the first goat, 'but I preferred the book.'

Why is it hard to talk with a goat around?
Because it butts in.

How does an octopus go into battle?
Well armed.

What did the beaver say to the tree?
'It was nice gnawing you.'

What's the correct name for a water otter?
A kettle.

What did the dog say when he sat on the sandpaper?
'Rough.'

'My dog's alive with ticks.'
'Well, don't overwind him.'

What happened to the cat that swallowed a ball of wool?
She had mittens.

What do you call a cat who sucks lemons?
A sourpuss.

Who tells chicken jokes?
Comedi-hens.

What happens to ducks that fly upside down?
They quack up.

How do you tell which end of a worm is the head?
Tickle its middle and see which end smiles.

What's the biggest ant in the world?
A gi-ant.

Why do bees hum?
Because they don't know the words.

What did the mother bee say to the naughty baby bee?
'Beehive yourself.'

What did the bee say to the flower?
'Hello, honey.'

What did one flea say to another?
'Shall we walk or take a dog?'

21 Clowning Around

If you want to make people laugh, doing silly things is as effective as telling silly jokes. This chapter is all about silly things to do. It tells you how to make a clown costume and face masks, how to do impersonations and ventriloquism, and ends with a collection of hilarious tongue-twisters which would get any ventriloquist's tang tonguelled up!

Clown costume

Everybody loves a clown and if you can get hold of a few old clothes, a hula hoop, some cardboard and some make-up you can create a very effective clown costume.

The clothes you will need are an old shirt, an old and over-large pair of trousers, and some braces, but if you cannot get all these, don't worry, because you can always improvise.

Pin the trousers round a small hula hoop using safety pins, and then suspend the hoop and trousers from the braces. You will then have a pair of large, bouncy trousers that will make everyone laugh. If they are much too long, roll the bottoms up so you don't trip over them.

If you want to create a pair of enormous shoes, then cut out four pieces of cardboard about 20 cm long by 15 cm wide and round off one of the shorter ends of each piece to give a toe shape. Stick two pieces of cardboard together with adhesive tape to make a kind of pocket that you can slip over your shoe, then do the same with the other two pieces. Colour the cardboard with felt-tip pens to match your shoes. Do take care when walking in your cardboard shoes, or you may trip over.

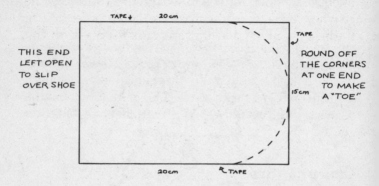

Put two pieces together with sticky tape on the three sides indicated.

Clown make-up

Colour your face white by patting flour on it. Then, with a red lipstick if you can borrow one, draw a red spot on each cheek, a red end to your nose, and a large red mouth. Borrow a dark eye pencil or eye shadow to draw in thick, exaggerated eyebrows, and if you like draw thin black lines from your upper eyelids to the eyebrows, and from your lower eyelids to about 2 cm down your face. Be careful not to poke the pencil in your eyes while doing this. If you want to be really theatrical, buy or make a wig out of long strands of wool to make floppy clown's hair. If you cannot manage to do this, then just stick a battered old hat on your head.

Nose masks

Take an ordinary, large-postcard-sized piece of cardboard and draw a funny face on it. Then cut out little,
unobtrusive holes for you to see through (they need not
be where the eyes on the mask are) and a larger hole for
the nose, as in the drawing, and stick the mask on your

face. If the nose hole is the right shape and size it will not
fall off but will give a very funny effect. You might try
looking like a clown, or a creature from outer space, or a
funny dog, or an old, old lady wearing spectacles, or a
man with a bushy beard.

Voice

The best way to learn to copy someone's voice is to take a tape recording of it if this is possible, and then play it over and over again and practise speaking like they do. You can test yourself with the recorder to check your progress. If you have no tape recorder then it is a question of listening hard and trying to reproduce what you hear. If your model has a marked accent or an unusually high- or low-pitched voice, then your task will be made easier.

Ventriloquism

It takes lots of practice to be a good ventriloquist, but if you want to have a go, then here are some tips to help you.

1.   Sit facing a mirror and try to speak without moving your lips. This is easiest to do if you keep your lips slightly apart rather than closing your mouth tightly.

2.   Take slow, deep breaths as you speak, trying to breathe out as you say something. This is called 'throw-

ing' your voice and will make it appear that the voice is coming from elsewhere rather than from you.

3. Try having a conversation with yourself, speaking in your normal voice and then in your ventriloquist's dummy voice.

4. Try speaking the individual letters of the alphabet without moving your lips. The most difficult letters are b, f, m, p and v, and it helps to press your tongue against the roof of your mouth when saying them.

5. The letter v can be substituted for b to help you at first.

6. The most difficult of the difficult letters are p and m so try and avoid words containing them.

Impersonations

If you can do good impersonations you may well have a future as a comedian! If you are serious about learning how to impersonate somebody, this is how you start.

Face

Study your model's face and then try and make yours look like it. You can make your face look fatter by padding out the insides of your cheeks with cotton wool; you could borrow some make-up and use an eye pencil to draw lines and wrinkles on your face, and rub a little talcum powder in your hair to give the appearance of greying.

Figure and clothes

It is difficult to make yourself look thinner but you can make yourself look bigger and fatter by putting a rolled-up towel across your shoulders under your jacket, and a cushion under your jumper. If you can borrow similar clothes to those worn by your model, so much the better, but if not you might be able to buy some cheaply in a charity shop.

Mannerisms

These, together with a person's voice and way of speaking, are the most important means by which they can be identified. If you copy them well enough then you will not need to pay too much attention to the clothes and make-up.

Watch the way your model walks and moves about. Do they take short strides or long ones? Do they move energetically or in a relaxed manner? Do they gesticulate with their hands while speaking? Do they have little habits you could copy, like scratching their nose or rubbing their chin? Are they right- or left-handed? It is important to note all these points so that you can reproduce them accurately.

Making a dummy

The easiest dummy to use is your hand! Clench your fist and tuck your thumb under your fingers. Move the

thumb up and down so it looks like a mouth. You can redden the mouth and draw in eyes with crayons or washable felt-tip pens. If you drape a handkerchief round the dummy's 'head' it will look like a little old lady in a headscarf.

If you have a willing friend, preferably one who is smaller than you, they could act as your dummy. Put two red dots on their cheeks and draw lines down at the sides of their mouth so it looks as if the lower jaw is hinged. Of course, you don't need to be a ventriloquist at all with this kind of dummy – you can cheat!

Knock, knock jokes (see Chapter 3) are great fun to try when you are practising your ventriloquism, and if you really want to make your audience laugh try 'teaching' your dummy to say the tongue-twisters listed below. But whatever act you do, remember that if you know you are not very good at it, try and do it really badly! Some of the funniest moments occur when things go wrong in a ventriloquist's act, and your incompetence may well end up keeping your audience in stitches!

Tongue-twisters to try

If you think any of these tongue-twisters are easy then try saying them several times over in succession and you may change your mind!

Red lorry, yellow lorry.

The Leith police dismisseth us.

Sheila Seethes sells Cheshire cheese, and shellfish that she shells and sells.

Mumbling bumblings. Bumbling mumblings.

That bloke's back brake-block broke.

A truly rural frugal ruler's mural.

Plain bun, plum bun, bun without plum.

Neil's knapsack strap snapped.

Roads close, so snow slows shows.

Shave a cedar shingle thin.

Cheryl likes cheap sea-trips on tripper ships.

The sixth sheikh's sixth sheep's sick.

Can you imagine an imaginary menagerie manager imagining managing an imaginary menagerie?

Esther tests siestas in Leicester.

Around the rugged rock the ragged rascal ran.

A pleasing place to place plaice is a place where plaice are pleased to be placed.

Will your Joe lend our Joe your Joe's banjo?

22 Classroom Chuckles

In this book you have seen how we make jokes about lots of different things – things that frighten us and make us feel insecure, people and situations we want to feel superior to, things that shock us. But I have so far omitted to mention another subject – perhaps the most obvious of all – about which we make jokes, and that is our familiar, everyday lives. For most of my readers most days of the year this means school, and that is why I have given jokes about school a special chapter of their own.

Jokes about school can take the form of witty replies to teachers' questions (the kind that would mean punishment if you ever dared utter them in class); incredibly stupid replies (which would probably have the same effect on teachers, as they would think they were being set up for a joke); and silly remarks by the teachers themselves. If you think about it you will realize that all these forms of school jokes have one thing in common – they illustrate the kind of scene we should all love to see at school but, on the whole, don't. Psychologists call this 'wish fulfilment', and I think it is why we all love jokes about the classroom. The pupils in the next ten jokes are all very cheeky, but don't you wish you could make remarks like these in your class?

HISTORY TEACHER: What was the Romans' most remarkable achievement?
MOLLY: *Learning Latin!*

HISTORY TEACHER: Why were the Dark Ages so called?

MILLIE: *Because they had so many knights.*

SCIENCE TEACHER: Name a deadly poison.

JOHNNY: *Aviation.*

SCIENCE TEACHER: Aviation?

JOHNNY: *One drop and you're dead.*

ENGLISH TEACHER: Darren, how do you spell 'elephant'?

DARREN: *E–l–i–f–a–n–t.*

ENGLISH TEACHER: That's not how the dictionary spells it.

DARREN: *You didn't ask me how the dictionary spells it.*

TEACHER: You can't sleep in my class!

ROLAND: *If you didn't speak so loud I could.*

TEACHER: You should have been here at nine o'clock.
SHEILA: *Why, what happened?*

PHYSICS TEACHER: Light travels at 186,000 miles an hour. Isn't that amazing?
ARTHUR: *Not really, it's downhill all the way.*

TEACHER: I wish you'd pay a little attention to what I'm saying.
BILL: *I'm paying as little as I can.*

GEOGRAPHY TEACHER: Where are the Andes?
BEN: *At the end of the armies.*

MATHS TEACHER: If you had £2.75 in one pocket and £5.32 in the other what would you have?
KEN: *Someone else's trousers.*

And here are ten jokes in which the pupils make very stupid replies indeed:

SCIENCE TEACHER: What is an atom?
PAUL: *A man who lived in the Garden of Eden with Eve.*

TEACHER: What is the Order of the Bath?
EDGAR: *Mum, Dad, then me.*

FORM TEACHER: What's your favourite subject, Carol?
CAROL: *Gozinta.*
FORM TEACHER: What's gozinta?
CAROL: *You know, two gozinta four, four gozinta eight . . .*

MATHS TEACHER: If I cut three oranges and four bananas into ten pieces each what would I have?
PETER: *A fruit salad.*

HISTORY TEACHER: When was Rome built?
DINAH: *At night.*
HISTORY TEACHER: Why do you say that?
DINAH: *Because Rome wasn't built in a day.*

ENGLISH TEACHER: Explain this sentence: 'Her beauty was timeless.'
PAT: *Her face could stop a clock.*

ENGLISH TEACHER: Give me an example of the use of the word 'fascinate'.
SALLY: *My raincoat has ten buttons but I can only fasten eight.*

BIOLOGY TEACHER: Where do fleas go in winter?
ANDREW: *Search me.*

BIOLOGY TEACHER: Name four members of the cat family.
SARAH: *Mother cat, father cat and two kittens.*

SCIENCE TEACHER: If we breathe oxygen in the day-time what do we breathe at night?

JANET: *Nitrogen?*

And here are some of those remarks that you wish your teacher had made:

A teacher walked into a classroom and spotted a boy sitting with his feet stuck out into the aisle. He was chewing gum. She called out, 'Alfred! Take that gum out of your mouth and put your feet in this minute!'

Then there was the teacher who asked his pupils which month had twenty-eight days in it.

Little Jimmy had a habit of going out of the room during lessons and not returning. One day he had reached the door when the teacher spotted him. 'Jimmy,' she cried, 'come back here!'

'Please, miss,' said Jimmy, 'I need to leave the room urgently.'

The teacher relented. 'Very well,' she said. 'But if you don't come back I shan't let you go again.'

Mrs Beasley was having difficulty in controlling her class. 'Will you all be quiet until I've finished explaining!' she shouted. 'Every time I open my mouth some idiot starts talking!'

It was the day the Junior School broke up for the winter holidays, and they were very excited. 'Please, miss, is it going to snow?' they chorused. 'Please, miss, look out of the window and tell us what the weather's like!'

The teacher looked out of the window. 'I can't tell you what the weather's like,' she replied. 'It's too foggy to see.'

A teacher at a rather smart school was trying to correct her pupils' table manners. 'One day you will all be young ladies,' she said, 'and young ladies never crumble their bread or roll in their soup.'

And of course, there is the classic:

'Keep silent when you are talking to me!'

Why not try and write a list in your book of things you wish one of *your* teachers had said?

23 Headgear

I'm delighted to announce that recently an entirely new kind of joke has sprung up. When, in 1984, as editor-in-chief of *Crack It!*, a puzzle and jokes magazine, I launched a crusade to find a new type of joke I must admit I was a bit dubious about finding one. What I was after was a completely new category of joke, like the elephant joke, the doctor joke, or the waiter joke – and what I discovered was the 'headgear' joke. Have you come across it? The original joke was:

What do you call a man with a spade on his head?
Doug.

This soon led to:

What do you call a man without a spade on his head?
Douglas.

And:

What do you call a man with a plank on his head?
Edward.

What do you call a man with two planks on his head?
Edward Woodward.

What do you call a man with a toilet on his head?
John.

What do you call a woman with two toilets on her head?
Lulu.

What do you call a man with a seagull on his head?
Cliff.

What do you call a man with a sewing machine on his head?
Fred.

What do you call a man with a crane on his head?
Derek.

What do you call a woman with a cat on her head?
Kitty.

What do you call a man with a paper bag on his head?
Russell.

157

What do you call a man with a black smudge on his head?
Mark.

What do you call a woman with a Christmas tree on her head?
Carol.

What do you call a man with a bag of soil on his head?
Pete. (i.e. Peat.)

What do you call a man with a poster on his head?
Bill.

What do you call a man with a car on his head?
Jack.

What do you call a man with a number plate on his head?
Reg.

What do you call a man with hay on his head?
Rick.

What do you call a man with a beach on his head?
Sandy.

   Those are the straightforward ones. Those that follow get cleverer and cleverer (or more and more awful!) and are intended to inspire you to create some of your own. They are, of course, all based on puns.

What do you call a woman with a radiator on her head?
Anita.

What do you call a man with bamboo on his head?
Cain.

What do you call a woman with a solicitor on her head?
Sue.

What do you call a woman with tiles on her head?
Ruth.

What do you call a man with a pot of paint on his head?
Hugh. (i.e. Hue – a colour.)

What do you call a man with a Marks and Spencer's cardigan on his head?
Wally.

What do you call a woman with an oyster on her head?
Pearl.

What do you call a man with very short hair on his head?
Sean. (i.e. Shorn – cut short.)

What do you call a man with a shroud on his head?
Paul. (i.e. Pall – a cloth spread over a coffin.)

What do you call a man wearing a notice on his head that says 'The End'?
Saul. (i.e. 'That's all'.)

But it's not quite the end. The headgear joke has sparked off some developments of its own:

What do you call a man wearing two raincoats in a cemetery?
Max Bygraves.

How many more can you think up?

24 The Best – and Worst – Jokes in the World

One of the joys of jokes is that their appeal is very personal – one person's favourite may not make another person laugh at all. I have spent many happy years collecting jokes and I decided to end this book with twenty of the best, and twenty of the worst, from my collection. Sometimes I like the best best and sometimes I like the worst best – and that's another thing about jokes – whether or not you find them funny depends on your mood. I'll leave you to make your own judgements about these. Here are the twenty that (on most days) I consider the gems of my collection:

How do you make a Swiss roll?
Push him off the top of an alp.

How do we know that Moses wore a wig?
Because he was sometimes seen with Aaron and sometimes without.

JUDGE: Constable, do you recognize this woman?
CONSTABLE: *Yes, m'lud. She approached me when I was in plain clothes and tried to pass this twenty-pound note off on me.*
JUDGE: Counterfeit?
CONSTABLE: *Yes, m'lud. She had two.*

What do you feed to baby gnomes to make them grow big and strong?
Elf-raising flour.

An Eskimo mother was sitting in her igloo reading a bedtime story to her small son. 'Little Jack Horner sat in a corner . . .'

'Mum,' interrupted the boy, 'what's a corner?'

Which king of England invented the fireplace?
Alfred the Grate.

How do you make gold soup?
Put fourteen carats in it.

'Doctor, doctor, every bone in my body aches.'
'Just be thankful you're not a herring.'

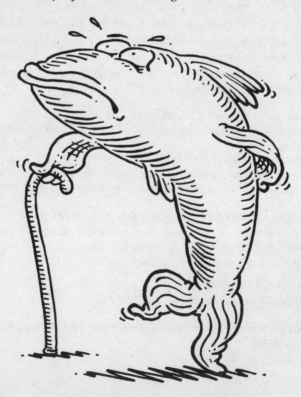

What do you call a Scotsman who delivers school meals?
Dinner Ken.

What's the difference between a buffalo and a bison?
You can't wash your hands in a buffalo.

What goes up a bell-rope wrapped in greaseproof paper?
The lunchpack of Notre Dame.

Why wasn't Eve afraid of catching measles?
Because she'd Adam.

Who has a parrot that shouts, 'Pieces of four! Pieces of four!'?
Short John Silver.

What did the earwig say as it fell out of the window?
''Ere we go.'

How does a ghoul begin a letter?
Tomb it may concern.

What did the baby hedgehog say as it backed into a cactus?
'Is that you, Mother?'

What did one caterpillar say to another when they saw a butterfly?
'You'd never get me up in one of those things!'

What's yellow, brown and hairy?
Cheese on toast dropped on the carpet.

What has 100 legs and cannot walk?
Fifty pairs of trousers.

What do you call two spiders who have just got married?
Newly webs.

And here are those that I consider the silliest, most groan-making jokes ever:

FIRST WOMAN WITH PRAM: I'm going to call my baby Orson, after Orson Welles.
SECOND WOMAN WITH PRAM: *What's your surname?*
FIRST WOMAN WITH PRAM: Cart.

LULU: Do you like my new swimming pool?
MABEL: *It's beautiful. But why isn't there any water in it?*
LULU: I can't swim.

Cuthbert noticed his neighbour, Egbert, looking very hard for something in the front garden.

'Lost something, Egbert?' he asked.

'Yes,' said Egbert. 'My spectacles.'

'Where did you last see them?' inquired Cuthbert.

'In the living room,' replied Egbert.

'Then why are you looking for them out here?' asked Cuthbert.

'There's more light out here,' said Egbert brightly.

BARBARA: I thought you were going water skiing.
BRENDA: *I was, but I couldn't find a sloping lake.*

CLARA: I used to take the bus to school every day.
CLAUDE: *Why don't you now?*
CLARA: My mother made me take it back every night.

BARRY: What have I got in my hands?
LARRY: *A double-decker bus.*
BARRY: You peeped!

BERT: Police in Manchester are looking for a bloke with one eye called Gerald.

FREDA: *What's his other eye called?*

JUDGE: Are you the counsel for the defence?

MAN IN COURT: *No, I'm the bloke that stole the bicycle.*

I have a green nose, three red eyes and four purple ears. What am I?
Very ugly.

GEOGRAPHY TEACHER: What is the climate of New Zealand?

KEVIN: *Very cold, sir.*

GEOGRAPHY TEACHER: Why do you say that?

KEVIN: *Because when they send us meat it arrives frozen.*

FATHER: Ben, why do you have a black eye?

BEN: *I bruised two fingers knocking in a nail in the carpentry class.*

FATHER: But your fingers look all right and it doesn't explain the black eye.

BEN: *Oh, yes, it does. They weren't my fingers.*

Aunt Agatha had bought herself a new, rear-engined foreign car. She took her old friend Gertrude out for a drive, but after a few miles the car broke down. The two women got out and lifted the bonnet. 'Oh dear,' said Gertrude, 'you've lost your engine!'

'Never mind,' said Aunt Agatha, 'I've got a spare one in the boot.'

CUSTOMER: A pound of stewing steak, please, and make it lean.

BUTCHER: *Certainly, madam, which way?*

CHARLIE: How many fish have you caught today?
EUSTACE: *When I get another I'll have caught one.*

PETE: This match won't light.
DAVE: *That's funny. It did this morning.*

JULIA: How do you spell 'erbert?
DAD: *You mean Herbert, don't you?*
JULIA: No, 'erbert. I've got the H down already.

BELINDA: I love the sun, don't you?
JEMIMA: *Oh, yes. I could sit in the sun all day and all night.*

STRANGER: What's the quickest way to the station?
LOCAL: *Running.*

DARREN: Mum, can I go out and play?
MOTHER: *What, in those clothes?*
DARREN: No, in the park.

MATHS TEACHER: Carol, your figures are so bad that an eight looks like a three.
CAROL: *It is a three, miss.*
MATHS TEACHER: Then why does it look like an eight?

And that is my very last awful joke, I promise you. I have to stop now, because, as the dirt said when it rained, if this lasts much longer my name will be mud!

Have a jolly, joke-cracking time!

Answers to catchphrases quiz Chapter 2

1. Larry Grayson
2. Frank Carson
3. Jim Davidson
4. Roland Rat
5. Jimmy of the Krankies
6. Cannon and Ball
7. Ken Dodd
8. Leslie Crowther
9. Stu Francis
10. Basil Brush.

Some other Puffins

THE HA HA BONK BOOK
Janet and Allan Ahlberg

This joke book is full of good jokes to tell dads, mums, baby brothers, teachers and just about anybody else you can think of.

MY SECRET FILE
John Astrop

A cross between a file, a diary and a suggestions book. Sample subjects include an IF page (If I could live anywhere, I'd live . . .) and a Christmas presents page (got what? gave what?).

Johnny Ball's THINKBOX

Johnny Ball, whose TV shows have made maths a popular subject with millions of children, shares his enthusiasm for numbers in these fascinating books of puzzles, tricks and brain teasers.

THE ANIMAL QUIZ BOOK
Sally Kilroy

A heavily illustrated quiz book covering all kinds of animals, birds, insects and reptiles. The first sections of the book are general ones, i.e. quizzes about the proper names for animal homes, animal young, masculine/feminine, markings and camouflage, countries of origin, biggest-smallest-fastest, etc. Later sections refer to specific animals, i.e. everything you could want to know about an elephant.

NUMBER GAMES
Kirsch & Korn

A lively book of number puzzles, games and tricks. Original and amusing illustrations.

A BOOK OF BOSH
Edward Lear

Edited by Brian Alderson, here is an unusual collection of Learical lyrics and Puffles of Prose, put together to display a wide range of Bosh both well known and lesser known. As well as limericks and nonsense songs, there are egg-strax from his letters and a dictionary of his wurbl inwentions.

THE PUFFIN JOKE BOOK
Bronnie Cunningham

Jokes, fun, nonsense, witticism, one thing and another, thrown together by the ingenious Bronnie Cunningham and scribbled all over by the inspired Quentin Blake. Try it on yourself and friends – you will be surprised.

THE PUFFIN BOOK OF BRAINTEASERS
Eric Emmet

Help Professor Knowall with his collection of puzzles.

THE CALENDAR QUIZ BOOK
Barbara Gilgallon and Sue Samuels

The lively and inventive quiz book which uses the months and special days of the year as a framework on which to hang a wide variety of questions – not just testing general knowledge but encouraging readers to find things out for themselves.

THE PUFFIN BOOK OF INDOOR GAMES
Andrew Pennycook

A stimulating selection of games, 75 in all, divided into six main areas: card games, dominoes, board games, dice, pencil and paper games, and match games. Graded in difficulty within each section with clear explanations, helpful diagrams and amusing cartoons, this will be the ideal book for those at a loose end and those who simply love games.

THE CRACK-A-JOKE BOOK

The 1,000th Puffin and a special book of jokes sent to The Goodies by children. For children of all ages.

THE END
Richard Stanley

Packed full of the best worst jokes, loathsome limericks and pathetic poems, this book is a groan-a-minute.

DAGGIE DOGFOOT
Dick King-Smith

Born the weakling of the litter, lucky to survive his first few days, Daggie Dogfoot becomes the only swimming pig in existence . . . and then sets his heart on mastering another form of locomotion.

FREAKY FRIDAY
Mary Rodgers

The funny and fast-moving story of how thirteen-year-old Annabel Andrews copes with the problems of being her own mother for a day!

WHO, SIR? ME, SIR?
K. M. Peyton

Sam Sylvester's class couldn't believe their ears when he calmly announced that he had entered them for a competition against the poshest school in the neighbourhood. And when they heard what kind of competition it was – tetrathlon – and who was in his team, they practically fell through the floor.